The Silence of Silver

Bridget Leanne
Carl Joseph Cascone

Copyright Page

**Published in the United States of America
by Pewter Publishing**

First Printing, 2019

ISBN 978-1-7338524-1-8

Acknowledgments

Carl- I have to acknowledge Bridget for her strength and dedication to this project. Also, my children Carl Vincent and Alyna Marie for their energy and motivation in my life. And my love to all three for helping me prove that once you separate yourself from negativity and drama, beautiful things can happen in your life.

Bridget- I want to acknowledge both of my parents, Pat and Becky Stoliker, for always supporting me and showing me what hard work and dedication can bring. I want to acknowledge my son, Cole. If we weren't for you, none of this would be possible. You pushed me to better myself and fight for a life we both deserve. My last acknowledgment goes to Carl. Without your guidance and support this story would never have come to life. You showed me my potential and for that I will forever be grateful.

We both also want to thank Lili Booth for her help with editing and formatting, Alexander Van Ness for the beautiful cover and anyone else that had a hand in creating this story.

Dedication

Carl would like to dedicate his contribution to this book to his Grandparents, Carl and Mary Caronite, for their endless love and encouragement.

Bridget would like to dedicate her contribution to this book to her twin sister, Brittany, for being the best hype woman and always seeing the potential in a crazy pipe dream.

The Silence of Silver

The First Collaborative Novel
by
Bridget Leanne
Carl Joseph Cascone

Chapter 1

Sitting in a room at Hope Covenant Long Term Care Facility, trying to pay attention to anything but the white nothingness of modern-day health care and the smell of overly floral cleaners, Frannie Plata thought about how she got here. Where did she go wrong? How did her incredible love story turn from a lifetime of romance with her one and only Hector, to a shared experience with doctors, nurses and the occasional lawyer? If you were to ask Frannie to explain her life in three words, she would only be able to give you one; Devoted. She was devoted to everything in her life; her family, her husband, her job and her friends. Anything Frannie did, she did to the best of her ability which is why, after almost two years of trying, her faith in her husband started to falter. It wasn't that Frannie loved Hector any less; it wasn't that he had done anything wrong, and it wasn't even that she was tired. Simply put, Frannie was out of ideas and the only thing she could do was focus on her routine as she did day in and day out, with a smile on her face, and devotion in her heart.

The love story between Frannie and Hector started like many others, but unlike the others, there was no driving force pushing them apart. There was no bad history between their families and there certainly was no poisonous death scene. In all reality, the two were perfect for each other and their families fully supported that. There were no objections at their wedding, there were no Christmas party fights or 4th of July barbecue brawls. The families got along in an impossible storybook fashion.

Growing up in the suburbs of Detroit sounds a lot rougher than it actually was. Hector and Frannie's families were neighbors in a small cul-de-sac, about 45 minutes outside the city. Frannie, her sister Maria and their brother Angelo, Hector and his brother Diego along with the other neighbor kids bonded over late night games of "Kick the Can" and "Hide N' Seek" that took up the entire block. During the summers it was hard for any of their parents to convince the kids to come inside for dinner, so all of the families ended up having large picnics in alternating yards, sharing hours of laughter, joy and the not-as-rare-as-you'd-think tears. Through these hours, Frannie and Hector grew closer, and because they were growing closer they pushed each other away. In high school, they both had relationships, they both had heartbreak and they both discovered themselves always going back to the "What If". It wasn't until Hector had come back from a failed go at traditional college that they really began to explore the relationship that always simmered below the surface.

By 1983, Hector, a reliable 22-year-old man with a tall, wide frame and thick black hair that fell around his tanned, square jaw and Frannie, a bold 20-year-old woman who stood a full 12 inches shorter, with raven black hair, porcelain skin and blue eyes you could swim in, were married in a beautiful, ruffle filled wedding that only the Eighties could produce. Dancing to Journey's "Faithfully" Frannie and Hector repeated their vows to each other, "Till death do us part." The love and kindness that emanated from the couple were feelings that made romance writers write and devout ballad singers sing. Just two years after their wedding, they welcomed a ball of energy named Angelo, after Frannie's father and brother. While Angelo wasn't exactly in the plans for Frannie and Hector at that moment, they took on the challenge head on and like most other stories, they were loving and caring parents. Despite the run around that Angelo had given them, after two more short years, another baby boy, Dominic, joined them and 3 years after that, a little baby girl named Gianna rounded out their perfect family. It was everything Frannie and Hector could wish for. A full family of five meant that Frannie stayed home with the children until they grew older. After that, she started a part-time job at a local elementary school as an aid to help children with behavioral issues and Hector worked at a car manufacturing plant. Frannie loved being a mother and flourished when others would wilt. She volunteered at their schools, over-decorated for every holiday and had home cooked meals on the table almost every night.

Their lives went on through the years like any typical Midwest family. There were school plays, birthday parties, and sweltering, humid summers were spent vacationing in Northern Michigan while winters were spent buried in feet of snow with below zero temperatures. The whole family used to go to places like the Detroit Zoo, Cedar Point and Greenfield Village to spend time together but that stopped shortly after the accident that left Hector trapped inside himself. Frannie tried to keep things going, to keep things as normal as she could, as to not disrupt the lives of her children and grandchildren but as much as she would have loved to enjoy those times, it became very clear that her heart was not in them. There was no sparkle behind her eyes or smile anymore, and everyone knew it was because Hector wasn't around.

In a room that smells way too sweet and is anything but cozy, her thumb rubbing Hector's arm, Frannie waited for Patty, a short, rounded woman that looked younger than she actually was, to come back with some information on her husband's improvements, if there were any. After two years, Frannie was losing all hope that her husband would fully recover from the forklift accident he was involved in at work, but she did have hope that one day he would wake up. While Hector couldn't move, speak or see, he had brain activity. Regular tests gave Frannie hope that Hector would wake up and besides needing some physical therapy, he would be the same man she fell in love with decades ago. She pushed the accident out of her mind like she did every time it popped up, which had been getting less and less frequent. This was a relief as well as a pang of tremendous guilt that Frannie had been struggling with because in her mind, who forgets that their husband is lying unresponsive in a hospital bed? She couldn't focus on her new source of anxiety just yet, she had to hear the news that she's been waiting for every day, which was no news. She had been told over and over again that no news was good news, that at least Hector wasn't getting any worse and because he wasn't getting any worse, that meant there was potential for him to get better.

"Everything still looks the same, Fran; you know what I'm going to say next." Patty walked around the medical bed that had a full rail on each side, something completely unnecessary since the entire year that Hector had been it in, he had never moved a muscle and smiled down at him, "He's not getting worse, which is a good sign, even after all this time. The only thing I can encourage you to do is just what you're already doing." Frannie gave Patty a smile and held onto Hector's arm, even though it looks like it shouldn't be, it was warm and something Frannie missed around her.

"All right, well…you know, if anything changes while I'm not here…" Frannie began but was cut off by Patty.

"I know Fran, we're all watching him, and he's in the best hands." Patty walked over to the side of the bed that Frannie was on, patted her shoulder and adjusted Hector's bed. That's all that was needed to be said. The same conversation happened day after day, a routine that both the women have fallen into a comfortable habit with. Frannie would go to work, leave at the same time every day and go straight to Hector. Frannie watched Patty as she walked across the threshold, closing the door behind her then turned back to Hector.

She watched, wishing his eyelids would twitch, willing them to open and show his beautiful brown eyes. She watched his chest move up and down in a slow, steady rhythm with the help of the machines he had been attached to. The humming in the room never seemed to go away and while at first, Frannie felt silly talking to someone that couldn't respond, she had grown used to hearing her own voice echo off the walls and imagined that Hector could actually hear her. This single thought is what kept her coming back, every day, to tell him about their family, her job, and anything else that came to mind.

She desperately tried to keep things as normal as they could be because, in her mind, Hector knew she was there and she wasn't ready to let that thought go. Doctors and nurses all smiled at her and no one had told her to stop or that she was wasting her time. They all encouraged her to continue to talk to him as if he could respond. It took some getting used to and some serious mental strength to feel as crazy as Frannie did while she babbled on and was the only coherent one in the room.

"Hi my love, I guess no news is good news, right?" She rolled her eyes. "I keep being told that and I don't know how long I'm going to believe it."

"I know baby, I know, just trust them, I'm right here...I hear you, I promise."

Right now seems like a good time in the story to let you in on a secret. Not a secret anyone is keeping intentionally but a secret nonetheless. While on the outside Hector seemed unresponsive, on the inside, he was trapped. He heard everything, had thoughts and emotions but lived in a body that couldn't express any of them. Due to his extensive injuries from the forklift accident, Hector was put into a medically induced coma. He was given dozens of different medications to help save him and although the medications, along with the machines, kept him alive, the mix had paralyzed Hector's body. Hector could feel and hear his wife, but he couldn't respond. After a year of fighting, Hector had to come to terms with the fact that he would never be able to kiss, talk to or hug his wife again. All he could do was cherish the time he had with her and fight to just open his eyes, even a little. Without the help of the machines and the medicines that had been constantly flowing into his veins, he knew he would die. A few months into the coma, the doctors unhooked the IVs and machines because they thought his body was healthy enough to pull out of the coma but to the distress of everyone involved, Hector didn't wake up, physically at least.

"Anyway, I saw the boys this morning; Sage has them wearing these....amber necklaces? Something about the calming power it has on the child. You know, hippy-dippy shit but..."

"Frannie, you have to trust her...both boys are happy, I know they are."

Hector thought while trying to will his arm to move towards her.

Frannie rolled her eyes again and took a deep breath. "Angelo tells me to trust his wife, even if I don't agree or understand what the hell she's doing. Both the boys are alive and happy, that's all I..." she stopped and looked down, "...we can ask for." She got up, walked over to the counter to grab a glass of water and took a drink. She leaned back and looked over to the man hooked up to a dozen different machines and monitors, realizing that the only familiarity between that man and her husband was a body that wouldn't move. She took another deep breath, something she had read online to do when you felt the panic rising in your throat. Frannie moved towards the bed, leaned over it to kiss her husband's forehead and smooth his hair that had grown way too long for his liking. She smiled at him, talking more too herself than to him, "I should get someone in here to cut this hair; he would have a heart attack if he saw how long it's gotten."

"I don't know, I think I kind of like it. The chicks dig my luscious locks. I may keep it if I'm able to get up again"

Hector thought as he relished in the feeling of his wife's fingers in his hair. He missed everything about her and being trapped in his own body was like watching her through a camera lens, yelling at the TV screen that all she had to do was look back and see that he was there the whole time. Hector tried with everything he had to get his hand to move closer to her but just like every other day, nothing moved, and no news was good news.

Chapter 2

Hector lay in his bed, stirring in the dark emptiness around him. He knew no one was in the room, only because he'd gotten used to the tiny crunch of a rusty hinge that happened when the door was pushed open. He knew he had been moved into a long-term care facility and while he had no idea what his room looked like, he knew every sound and smell. He knew that there had to be a tree outside his window because at night when everything is quiet, he heard the faint scratching against the glass. He knew that the floors were tiled by the way the nurse's tennis shoes squeaked and he knew that his life was wasting away with the repetitive ticking of the clock on the wall to his right that never seemed to let up. When he was alone, all he had were his own thoughts and the clock, mocking him, letting him know that every second he is in that bed, is a second away from his wife and his family.

While Hector thought the sounds taunted him, it was the smells that did so even more. It wasn't the medical smells that you would initially think would bother someone. Hector got used to the cleaners they used throughout the facility. It was the smell of his wife that tormented him the most. He knew exactly when she walked into the room by the way the air around him shifted and the smell of her perfume that he knew she applied behind her ears and on her wrists wafted into his nose. In the 35 years they had been married, the smell of his wife always drove him nuts in the best way possible.

He remembered a time shortly after they were married, at the grocery store preparing for their first time hosting Christmas dinner. Frannie was walking, looking down at the list and next to Hector while he pushed the cart when she almost passed up an item that she needed; Marshmallows. Instead of going around Hector, she reached past him, over the cart to grab a bag of the mini marshmallows for her sweet potato casserole and when she did, Hector nuzzled his nose in her neck and inhaled, never wanting to forget the scent of his beautiful bride, the perfect mixture of lilac and white linen. At that moment, Frannie smiled to herself, loving Hector's small signs of affection and threw her marshmallows into the cart. With the 12 inch difference in height between the two of them, Frannie had to look up to meet his eyes but when she did, he couldn't help but scoop her up into an embrace, pushing his nose back into her neck and growling.

His daydream stopped then as he heard the hinge on the door open and the familiar squeak of tennis shoes. He wasn't sure who it was yet, but he knew it was someone medical and not his family or friends by the pace of the shoes. They were there to get in and get out as if he wasn't even there. He heard the person to the right of him and instantly he knew it wasn't his normal nurse, Patty. Patty hummed a soft melodic tune while she walked that put Hector instantly at ease and was so low that he only heard it when she was right next to him. This woman was in a rush so he knew it had to be someone new. Not once did this new nurse acknowledge him, not once did she speak to him and while he grew frustrated, he understood it. Would he have talked to someone that supposedly couldn't hear you? Would he have gone out of his way to make someone lying in a hospital bed, unresponsive, feel better? Probably not and he knew that it was only human to ignore those not making a fuss.

Hector knew that his situation could be much worse. He could have a family that gave up on him three days into his coma, he could be waiting day after day for a visitor to come and he could actually be going through what the doctors thought he was going through. Instead, Hector had his mind, and both a blessing and a curse, he couldn't help but be thankful that he could experience whatever he could while he still was alive. He knew this wouldn't last forever and he knew that he could die at any moment, every possible situation running through his mind. There could be a power outage, the generator could stop working and he would die a slow, painful death or a tornado could blow through the city, ripping up the roof above his head, breaking his window and sucking him out. He even imagined his death in impossible situations just to break up his days.

His favorite being crushed by the foot of Godzilla. Imagining the ways he would die took up a lot of time, whether they were realistic or not, but he always imagined waking up and what he would say to his wife, who would conveniently be sitting next to him, with her sweet smile and a bottle of his favorite beer. He created narratives of his life, where he woke up and fully recovered from whatever was happening to him. He would run around with his grandkids, help his wife cook Sunday dinners and go back to work, being a productive member of society instead of a leech, sucking the joy and money from the people that mattered most to him.

There were a million things that Hector would say was the worst about being trapped inside his paralyzed body, on the top of his list, was the guilt that he felt, knowing that every day his wife sacrificed the closure she could have if he had died that day or the time she spent talking to someone that would never respond to her. He felt guilty about draining the savings account they worked so hard to build up for retirement. He felt guilty about leaving her the way he did, about the mundane kiss he gave her the morning of his accident or the quick "Love you!" he yelled on his way out the door. He felt guilty that his grandkids wouldn't remember him, especially Angelo's youngest one, Buzz, who was just a small baby when he left them and he felt guilty for all the time he spent wishing he would just die.

Life had been something that Hector cherished but he definitely took it for granted, like millions of other people. He never thought something like this would happen to him but then again, no one ever does. A life of just your mind is a life that Hector struggled to accept. He struggled to come to terms that it was this or death and while most of the time he chose to be there for his wife, even if she didn't know it, he had slipped into some dark thoughts when the pain was too much or the loneliness took over. He thought of the times when just the pressure of Frannie's hand on his would be too much to handle and no matter how hard he tried to scream or move, he just had to accept the pain and accept his fate.

There were definitely dark times in Hector's new life but that's not to say there weren't good ones too. He loved when he heard the pitter-patter of little feet running down the hallway towards his room and the abrupt noise tornado that spun closer and closer. He loved when his grandchildren came to visit him even though he knew they didn't fully understand the situation. His children came to visit often but it was mostly his daughter-in-law, Sage, that brought in her and Angelo's boys. With her freckled face, a flowered headband over her long red hair and her slight physique she always brought some sort of holistic medicine that she swore would help Hector wake up, usually, a smelly one but Hector welcomed anything new. His grandsons would get into his bed with him while Leaf, the older of the two and a spitting image of his father at that age, would tell him about his day in the nature-based preschool he was going to. Hector learned that at even 4-years-old, Leaf was learning to farm and raise chickens; he was learning about the seasons by being out in them and experiencing everything firsthand. When Hector's kids were young he would have never thought about putting them in Leaf's school, let alone any preschool but right now he was thankful for the experiences the boys were getting.

Sometimes they got a little rowdy and Sage had to take them home after only a few minutes but Hector would take anything he could get. His daughter, Gianna, a gorgeous female version of her father, often came to visit as well, bringing along her 6-year-old son Roberto. Roberto, or as Hector called him, Bobby, was the oldest of the grandkids and looked like an out of place Viking with blond hair and green eyes that he inherited from a dad that was no longer around and was the most reserved. He'd had trouble in the beginning, seeing his grandpa hooked up to machines and not really showing any real signs of being alive. He wasn't sure how to act around him, if he should be scared of him or if he could hear anything that Bobby was saying. With a little gentle nudging from his mother and grandmother, Bobby soon fell into the same routine that Frannie did. He would talk to his grampa as if he were having a conversation. He told Hector about starting 1st grade and how he had made some new friends on the playground.

When Gianna would leave the hospital room, Bobby would even tell Hector about the girl he liked in school, what her name was, the color of her hair and the way she teased him in class. This always made Hector smile, or at least try to smile. He loved that even though he couldn't respond to his grandson, he was still that person Bobby could confide in. In that moment, Hector hoped that if he were ever able to get out of this bed that the dynamic between him and this child that had grown up in front of his ears wouldn't change. He promised himself that when that day came, he would take Bobby golfing, they would eat chili dogs and get bottles of Coke after the ninth hole and Bobby would know that he could always look up to his grandfather.

In Hector's life two things remained consistent; His love for his family and the love of music. Hector took every opportunity to play music for his family, whether it was live from his guitar or songs from his past on the radio. Hector loved being able to share the universal language with whoever would listen. Between the kids running around with their friends, the music coming from the radio or the guitar that Hector attempted to teach all of his children but was never successful, the house was always loud. Lying day after day in a sterile, quiet room was enough to break him but he took anything he could and turned it into music, which is one of the many reasons why Hector loved the rain. In his mind, he heard each raindrop hitting the glass window as a music note. He heard when the drops combined to make chords and he heard the chords combine, softly playing his latest composition that he named "Rainy Day Music Box". It was one that he knew no one but he would ever hear. When the time came, if it did, for Hector to go back to his life, one of his goals was to write down his music. He wanted his children to be able to hear it, he wanted them to be able to play it and appreciate it as much as he did while lying motionless in his room.

Chapter 3

"I know you want to know more, Mrs. Plata, but there just isn't any new information. His workplace is dragging their feet on the incident report for the accident and technically, they are still within their window of time to give us this information. If I could hurry them along, I would." Frannie and her son, Angelo, the only one that somewhat resembled her, but with Hector's brown eyes, sat across the oversized and probably overpriced desk opposite of her lawyer. Robert Milano, a very average man in both height and weight with earlobes that hung lower than you would expect and the beginning of a very thin hairline continued, "I know this is hard to swallow and I know you feel like you're wasting your time, but I promise in the end, it'll all be worth it." The case that was set up against Hector's job was one that her oldest son had urged her to follow through on. Angelo thought it was necessary to sue them for the mounting medical bills. Frannie was not the confrontational type so when the word "Lawsuit" came into play, she wanted nothing to do with it. She knew that accidents happen in Hector's line of work and unfortunately, this one had happened to them. She tried to keep everything straight in her head and she tried to give Hector's job the benefit of the doubt, but the longer they went without helping out in the case, the more frustrated Frannie grew. Hector had worked for them since he was 22 and was a top performing employee. She couldn't imagine what could be taking them so long but her thoughts were interrupted by her son's outburst.

"We need them to start moving. My father is *still* lying in a hospital bed, almost two years later, wasting away and we know next to nothing about how he got there. How did it happen?! Why did it happen?! And why is no one cooperating?!" Angelo got upset every time he went to the law office but refused to let Frannie go alone. She knew that these meetings agitated Angelo, but she was grateful for his help and support when it came to the messy part of Hector's accident.

Robert, who was a great lawyer and had been treating Frannie and her family as if he actually cared, had been left with no other options. He was just as frustrated as they were and he tried his best to move the case along. "I'll contact their lawyer again and remind them of the deadline. It's a big company though, and sometimes they aren't the most cooperative, so just be prepared for the long road ahead of us, okay?" He tried to give them his best smile to reassure them in their case but it held little weight with Frannie. She was discouraged and didn't want to continue to frustrate her son but she knew she had to get down to the bottom of this. Frannie needed to know, after almost two years of waiting, why her husband is in a bed, his life completely stopped and no one has been able to tell her. She knew there was an accident, she knew that Hector had been crushed under parts, but she didn't know how those parts got there, she didn't know who was involved and she didn't know or understand the reason behind all the secrets. The three of them stood, shook hands and Frannie and Angelo left as Robert's phone started to ring.

It had been a tradition, if that's what you'd like to call it, that Frannie and Angelo went to lunch after meeting with the lawyer. There were talks that were needed, but that were hard to start and decisions to be made over hot dogs and salads at the local Coney Island Diner. The whole family would be asking Frannie and Angelo how it went and they liked to get all the facts together before taking it home to the rest of the bunch. While at this particular lunch date, Frannie's cellphone started to ring and she saw "Robert Milano" flash on the screen, which was strange, since they just left his office no more than an hour before. Hitting the green button on her phone, with a concerned look on her face, she answered, "Hi Mr. Milano. Is everything okay? Did we leave something at your office?" Angelo watched as his mother's face went from concerned, to confused and finally blank. He couldn't hear what the lawyer was saying, but he knew that his mother wasn't saying anything, only nodding her head, as if the lawyer could see her through the phone connection.

When she finally thanked him and put her phone down on the table, she took a moment to take a breath before looking across the table at her son. "That was the lawyer...he said that he got a little bit of information from the company's lawyer about the accident. Apparently, a forklift hit some racking and that fell, knocking over another rack, which hit your dad. A person caused this. This wasn't *just* an accident, this wasn't a freak thing. Someone caused it...someone took your father away from us and we *still* don't know why. Why are there so many secrets? It's been almost two damn years?! Why can't Paul help us?" Frannie had never remembered being as mad as she was at that moment. Paul was Hector's supervisor and longtime friend to both of them.

Hector and Paul started working at the factory at the same time and instantly grew close. They worked alongside each other for years until Paul was promoted to a supervisor and became Hector's boss. This didn't change their relationship, though. Paul and Hector were able to fall into a great working routine and Paul continued to attend Hector's family functions. Frannie never thought she could ever think badly of Paul and it made her sick to think that he knew what happened to her husband and wasn't cooperating with the investigation. This wasn't a freak accident, this wasn't something that happened on the job, this was an accident that was caused by someone and Paul had been there.

Angelo dropped his mother off at home, with a kiss on the cheek and watched her get into her car instead of going into the house. He knew instantly where she would be going. All Angelo could do was give his Mom a supportive smile, a wave and drive off towards his own home. He knew that he would have to tell his sister and brother about the new piece of information about his dad's case but he wasn't sure exactly how to do it. He almost felt stupid that after two years they were just now finding out that someone else had been involved. How could they not know that someone knocked over the rack? In all reality, the family never really asked WHY it happened, only about what happened, and what happened was known.

Angelo kicked himself mentally about not asking more questions in the beginning, for not being more on top of this. He knew his Mom had a lot going on and how she never wanted to start a lawsuit but for the sake of his father, he knew he had to move forward with it.

Frannie went into autopilot after Angelo dropped her off. She got into her car and drove. She drove straight to Hector. Walking into the facility it hit her that Hector might not have even known what happened to him. She pushed open his room door and took a few steps in. Frannie took in the sight in front of her, her husband who had once stood well over 6 feet tall now permanently horizontal. The arms that once held not only her, but also their children and grandchildren were now skinny and fragile. The face that had been full and plump from one too many desserts after dinner now looked as if it belonged to a completely different person. Frannie pulled a chair close to his bedside and ran a finger along the side of his face.

"My love, I have missed you."

Hector focused on the hand closest to Frannie, trying to feel every muscle in hopes that it would be able to caress the face of the woman he had loved his entire life. To his surprise, a muscle in his elbow twitched, enough for him to know he had moved but not enough for Frannie to notice.

"I moved...Frannie I moved! Please, please look down, look at my arm!"

"Hector, I wish I knew what was going on in that head..."

"I do too darling, I wish you knew I was here..."

"...I wish you could tell me what happened. The lawyer said that someone was behind your accident...that someone did this to you. That's it. That's all I know. I guess this is a case where no news isn't good news..."

"Of course someone did this; I just wish I knew who…I wish I knew why. Was it an actual accident?"

Hector thought constantly about his accident and played the events of the day over and over again but could never remember anything out of the ordinary. It happened like any other day, nothing stood out and nothing new happened.

"I just want to know what happened to you, I want to know why this happened to you. What did we do to deserve this? We aren't bad people…sure, we don't go to church like we should, we let our kids watch TV when they were younger, remember the time we left that case of pop on the bottom of our cart and accidentally walked out without paying for it? Was that it you think?" Despite herself, Frannie giggled. She knew that wasn't the reason this was happening but in her mind, she needed to blame it on something so why not their accidental shoplifting escapades?

"We didn't even realize we stole it until we got home! Do you remember that?"

"I remember my darling, you were freaking out."

"I didn't know what to do! I looked over the receipt like I always do and realized it wasn't on there...and you didn't care!" Frannie pushed Hector's shoulder a little with a smile on her face, leaving her hand there.

"I did care! I told you if you wanted to we could go back and pay for it. We shopped there all the time, no one noticed, neither did we, it wasn't a big deal you goofy woman."

"I guess I should have told you..." Frannie said with a small smile, "...I went back the next day and paid for it. I know it's silly but I just felt so bad, I couldn't make it through my day, I thought about it constantly!" What Hector would never be able to tell Frannie was that he knew she went back and paid for the case of pop because he went back to pay for it too. As soon as he rounded the corner into the store, he saw her, explaining the situation to the clerk and handing over the money. At that moment, he wanted to run to her and catch her in her do-gooding but he knew if she wanted him to know, she would have told him. All he could do was smile and hope she didn't see him as he left. "I should have told you. Maybe in some weird Karma way it didn't get to you because I never told you about it…is that a thing? Delayed Karma due to ignorant bliss? I hope not…" Frannie laid her head down on the bed, gently picking up Hector's hand and laying it against her face. She shut her eyes just as the tears started edging towards their descent over her cheeks, knowing that if she opened them, she would have to face the truth of the situation. In her head, she was able to imagine a time where Hector would have placed his hand against her cheek, a time where Frannie could relax, knowing that she had her life with Hector back. She stayed still a long time, rubbing the back of the hand that should have been running through her hair before breaking the silence,

"Hector, come back to me. You cannot leave me like this. You cannot quit your life." These few words fueled Hector's guilt about wanting to end his life.

"Baby, I haven't left you, I haven't quit. I wish you could see how hard I'm trying."

Feeling her cheek under his hand meant more to him than he thought it would. He felt the tears streaming down her face and if guilt and heartbreak could actually kill you, Hector's life would have ended right then. He got mad, he screamed in his head and he tried to fight but like almost every other time, nothing happened. His arms didn't wrap around his wife as he wanted to. His eyes didn't open to look at this woman whose heart was breaking right in front of him. His lips weren't moving to tell her how sorry he was that he left her, and how he never wants to be away from her again. Hector hated his life at that moment. He hated that he couldn't be there for the woman he vowed to always protect and he hated that he had to lie here, within inches of Frannie and unable do anything to soothe her cracking soul.

He got his muscle to twitch, that meant that he still had the ability to move or was it a fluke? Was it a coincidence that a muscle happened to twitch while he was trying to move or did he actually move it himself? Was he getting better? Would he wake up and go back to his life with his family and never take another day for granted? These thoughts gave Hector hope but he'd had hope before and he'd been let down. He couldn't continue on this journey without hope so as much as he wanted to give up, he didn't. He would continue to fight for his life, for his Frannie, and for his family. He could feel his body growing weaker, the muscles deteriorating every day. He could feel that he was dependent on these machines and the pain that he was feeling was getting worse. He wanted to live, for his family, but he was growing tired and knew that physically, his body would be shutting down soon, there was just no way to tell anyone that. The machines were picking up his heart rate, blood pressure and all the vitals he had but without being able to tell the doctors and nurses about the pain in his chest or the way that he feels as though even that the machines were working, he still was having a hard time breathing, they could never diagnose or fix the issues.

"Frannie, I wish I could tell you what was wrong, I wish you could hear me. I want to thank you for being here with me and tell you that I love you. I want you to hear me say those words to you and I want you to be able to get closure. I wish there were some way you could tell the doctors about my chest pain. Something else is wrong, something new. I don't know what though, and I can't tell anyone...I love you, my darling. I wish I could tell you that."

Frannie sat up, wiped the tears from her eyes and looked down at her husband, "I'm sorry, I know I need to be strong. I'm just so tired. I don't know what else to do. I don't know how to help you. I love you, Hector, I hope you know that..."

"I know that Fran, I will always know that. I just hope you know how much I love you and how much I wish I could be there with you, instead of stuck in my body."

Frannie chewed on her lip and rubbed Hector's arm before standing up. She knew that she needed to keep hope, that she needed to feel like there was something she could do but at this moment, that was a hard feeling to conjure. She kissed her hand and placed it on his head and walked out of the room, leaving a scent trail of her perfume behind her.

When Frannie got home, she ignored the messages on the landline that her children constantly teased her about still having and walked straight into the kitchen. Her purse hit the floor at the same time her keys hit the countertop and without skipping a beat, Frannie walked over to the cupboard and pulled out a wineglass. She never was a big drinker and the only reason she had wine in the house was that Gianna had come over a few nights ago with it to help her relax. It did the job until Frannie was in bed, alone, in a large house that used to hold so much laughter and so much excitement. Now, the half bottle of wine was calling her name from the fridge. She poured herself a decent amount and left it out on the counter, walking over to the sofa that held so many memories. She thought about the Christmas parties that were held here and the Thanksgiving dinners that had been hosted, the birthday parties and the sleepovers. Her house that had once been the hub for her family now mocks her for being so alone. While yes, her children and grandchildren come over to visit, it wasn't the same being here without Hector and she dreamed of the day that he would come through that front door again.

Frannie sipped on her wine, willing herself to cry or to scream, to express her emotions in some way but the truth for her was that she was empty. Frannie stared at the wall, nothing swimming in her head, nothing coming forward to remind her that she should be hysterical and nothing that produces the emotions people think she should have. After 22 months of her husband being asleep and kept alive only by machines, Frannie was giving up and the guilt that came along with that was enough to crush her. Frannie wanted to keep going, she wanted Hector to wake up, but here, alone at home, she could finally feel her true feelings. She was tired. She didn't know how long she could keep going. She had to pretend all day, through work, through lawyer and doctor appointments, in front of her family and even at the grocery store when she ran into an old friend or a neighbor. She never truly felt like she was in her body, just that she was always watching herself from across the room, wondering how she did it. She knew there were decisions that had to be made but that night; Frannie drank her glass of wine, took a hot shower and lay in her big bed, alone, preparing for the next day.

Chapter 4

June was a tough month for the Plata family. Not only was it Hector's birthday, but it was also very close to the anniversary of the accident, which had happened in the first week of July. The month was filled with dread and bittersweet memories of past birthdays. This June was the same as the first one, almost a year after the accident and Frannie felt as though she was always holding her breath. Hector's birthday would be June 8th and while Frannie didn't feel much like celebrating, the kids did. Gianna planned a dinner for the family at Frannie's house; she did the cooking and the decorating. Angelo, Sage and their boys showed up just before 6 o'clock while Gianna and Bobby had been there almost all afternoon. Sitting around the large dining room table, Frannie noticed that there were two empty place settings. Just then, she heard the front door opening and a booming voice traveling down the hall, "Helllllooo family! You don't have to wait any longer, we have arrived!" Frannie stood up as her hand instinctively flew to her chest, her middle son, Dominic, had flown in for his father's birthday. Dominic was the perfect mix of both Frannie and Hector with light skin and the dark hair that both of them had but Hector's big brown eyes. He lived in New York City with his partner, Derrick, an obvious New Yorker just from the way he carried himself. He had short black hair and Hector always described him as a much taller Al Pacino. Frannie loved both of them and couldn't believe what she was seeing. They usually made the trip in July but she was grateful they were here now. She ran over to the men and pulled them both into a bear hug, kissing both of their cheeks.

Derrick smiled and hugged Frannie back, "Hey, Ma. We missed you." All Frannie could do was hold them closer and wish she didn't have to let them go. Eventually, the group was broken apart by the little sticky hands of nephews wanting to see their uncles.

"Hey there fellas, whatcha all been up to?" Dominic questioned as he walked into the living room, the two older boys at his side and a redheaded Buzz toddling behind them, pulling on his brother's sleeve.

Frannie looked over at Gianna, both with tears in their eyes. Gianna knew her Mom and had seen how little Frannie was actually paying attention to life. She knew her mother had been distracted and she knew that things were changing. She wanted to give her Mom just a moment of peace with her children before the inevitable storm hit. Frannie crossed the room and took Gianna into her arms, hugging her tight and whispering, "Thank you."

Now that the table was full, food was being passed and laughter was in the air. Frannie listened to her children talk, for a brief moment not worrying about anything else until she heard Derrick speak up from the roar of conversation that Frannie couldn't possibly follow, "Dom, didn't you say your dad fell off a roof before? What was that story again? A birthday party or something?"

Dominic, Gianna, and Angelo all started laughing. When they finally caught their breath, Dominic started retelling the story, "Well, yes, Dad did fall off of a roof, after drinking just a little too much..." Frannie smiled to herself, being able to laugh about the incident two years later. The memories of that 4th of July party came flooding back into her head. The barbecue with all their friends and families, the Kamikazes that Hector had just learned to make and insisted on giving them to everyone. Like Frannie, Hector was also not a drinker but liked to have a beer here and there during parties but he had wanted this barbecue to be different. He researched the best Kamikaze recipe and had been perfecting his drink for weeks. Frannie was always his test subject and while she was surprised by how much better each drink was, she was getting sick of lime and vodka, which is why she declined to drink them at the party. Hector, on the other hand, drank lots of them. Every time he made one for someone else, he made one for himself and pretty soon, Hector thought he was the king of the world. Frannie actually enjoyed watching Hector let loose every once in a while. She smiled as she watched him run around the backyard with the kids, thinking to herself that he probably shouldn't be drinking this much in front of their grandkids and that tomorrow she would tell him that he needed to keep that away from them. Right now though, she let him have his fun.

Angelo had been in charge of the grill since Hector was otherwise indisposed and grilled up hot dogs for the kids, chicken, and hamburgers for the adults, corn on the cob and various other veggies. Now that the kids were older, these parties weren't as hard or stressful to host. Everyone brought dishes to pass, drinks to share and helped with the cooking and cleaning. Frannie was left to sit in one of the lawn chairs, a Diet Pepsi in her hand, watching her family in sheer bliss. Her favorite memory though was watching Hector sit across from 4-year-old Bobby and 2-year-old Leaf, trying to teach them how to whistle only to watch the two boys spit all over themselves. When Hector realized that whistling may be a little out of reach for the toddlers, he moved to ear wiggles. Most of the rest of the night was in fits of laughter after asking Bobby and Leaf to do grampa's special ear trick. They wiggled every part of their face but their ears and broke out into laughter when they saw they were entertaining the adults.

That bliss was quickly turned into concern when she heard her husband say "Boys! Do you want to play Frisbee?! I know where one is! On the garage roof! I'll get it for you!" and away Hector went, with determination on his face. Frannie jumped up to stop her very drunk, very wobbly husband from climbing the ladder up to the roof for a Frisbee that had been up there at least 10 years, since her boys were younger.

"Hector. Hector, stop. Look, I'll climb up and get it; you shouldn't be doing this right now." Frannie held onto his arm as he pulled the ladder from the garage. He set it up against the house and turned towards his wife.

"Aw, I'll be okay sweetheart, look at you…so concerned for me, so loving…so caring. Look at you." He said this while putting his hands on her face, squishing her cheeks together and making a kissy face. "I'll be okay Fran-Fran, promise. Hope to stick a needle in my eye and die, or…hope to die and stick a pencil…how does it go?"

Frannie couldn't help but laugh at her usually very sober husband and told him, "Then let me hold the ladder for you, please. I really don't want this to be happening but you aren't going to take no for an answer, are you?" But before Frannie could get her question out, Hector was already halfway up. All she could do was hold onto the ladder, as well as her breath. She looked around and saw that everyone was doing the same thing, just watching and waiting for Hector to get off of the roof. He successfully retrieved the Frisbee and threw it down to his grandsons without even so much as a stumble. It wasn't until he turned around to get back on the ladder that he put the wrong foot down, missing the ladder completely and falling the 8 feet down to the ground. A collective gasp came from behind

Frannie fell next to Hector, asking if he was all right. Almost immediately, a crowd formed around Frannie and Hector, the children who were waiting for their grampa to play with them, now surrounded his still body on the ground. At first, he didn't move and Frannie's heart sank but slowly she heard this gurgle coming from Hector's mouth. Frannie had no idea what was going on and she was ready to have someone call 911 but she realized that Hector was laughing. His laughter grew louder and louder, becoming contagious to the rest of the crowd, along with the relief that he was okay. The anger and fear that had shot through her body were slowly fading, even though she didn't join into the laughing fit that everyone else was in. He tried to move but she told him to sit still for a while, to make sure he wasn't actually hurt but Hector, being in the frame of mind that he was, waved her off and stood up with the help of Dominic, faking cracking his back. "Next time let me help you, okay old man?" Dominic wiped the grass off his dads back and rolled his eyes.

"Ahh! No need to go to a chiropractor. Just fall off the damn roof! I feel good as new!" With that, Hector was right back to playing with the kids, running around and throwing them into the air. Frannie sat in the grass in disbelief, willing her blood pressure to drop and trying to breathe. She knew that tomorrow he would be feeling the fall as well as the hangover but she also knew that tonight now called for one of Hector's Kamikazes.

"Was that the year the neighbor had the big fireworks show? When one of them fell over and started shooting at us?" Gianna had to ask this question because as Frannie remembered it she kept up with her father's drinking ability that night. "I think that's when we all had to get up and run away from them, right? Remember that camper caught on fire? Tommy Davidson's? He'd just gotten it out of storage to go camping that week, he had it all open to air out, perfect for potential firework housing." Gianna laughed at her own joke while the rest of the table laughed at the memory. Frannie thought of the fire now, seeing the crowd scatter and the fire truck use their yard to get close to the camper. No one was hurt and the fire was easily put out but it still ruined Tommy's camping trip.

"No, that was a couple years before that. This was only two years ago, remember? It was only a few days before dad's accident..." Dominic trailed off. The table died down for a moment, the only voices being heard were those of the kids. Frannie smiled a sad smile at her son, knowing that he felt guilty about not being around when his dad got hurt. Dominic came to visit for holidays and one trip in the summer. He had gone back home two days before Hector went into his coma. When Angelo called him to tell him the news, Frannie had told Angelo to tell him that he would be fine, and not to use the money for a plane ticket until Hector woke up, which should have been a few weeks after the accident. That was something that Frannie also regretted, telling Dominic to not come back. They made eye contact, gave each other a small smile and moved on with the conversation, Dominic turning to Gianna "The year the fireworks attacked might have been a few years before that. Wasn't Bobby like, a baby-baby?"

Gianna nodded, looking over at her child who now stood just over 4 feet tall. His big eyes were turned towards his Uncle Angelo, watching him cut food for his younger cousins. "Oh yeah, you're right. Bobby was very little, probably only a few months old. I remember panicking, thinking that he wouldn't make it to his first birthday."

The fireworks show that happened the year of the Kamikazes had gone off flawlessly. Lying on blankets in their front yard, the entire Plata family had their heads turned towards the night sky, watching the brightly colored sparks fly through the air. Hector had sobered up a little by then, the decision being somewhat Hector's idea but mostly Frannie's. After he fell off the roof, Frannie hid the other bottles of vodka, claiming that they were gone. Their blanket sat behind everyone else's so Frannie could watch the fireworks but also the little faces of her grandsons. She sat in front of Hector, between his legs and leaning back against his chest, feeling herself move with every breath he took. This was her happy place; this is where Frannie always wanted to be. She nuzzled her head back against Hector and felt his lips place a gentle kiss on the top of her hair. Smiling, she leaned her head back more to peek at him, his upside-down face smiling back down at her and his lips hitting her forehead. This was family. This was love. These Moments were the ones that Frannie always fantasized about. The Moments that would fit perfectly into a romance movie, a ballad playing in the background and a filter on the frame. Frannie wanted to hold onto this memory forever, never letting go of the thought of Hector, big, strong and happy.

It wasn't until she heard her oldest son calling her that she snapped out of her thoughts and realized she had tears falling down her face. Quickly she wiped them away, standing up to clean the table and push focus onto someone else. "Dominic, how is work going? Any cool new stories?" Dominic worked for an online blog in New York as a writer and while she normally would have loved to hear the answer, she had completely blocked out the voices of her children. She prayed that the memory of those fireworks made their way back to her mind and was disappointed when the only thought that came was to run away and hide. The rest of the table took notice of the sudden change in their mother and decided not to push her. They knew how hard she worked at making everyone else happy; how she always tried to hide her own feelings so as to not burden anyone else with them. Dominic turned to his siblings, telling them how his work had been going.

After dinner was over and the house started to clear Frannie was giving hugs and kisses at the front door, the pretend smile back on her face, the one she had grown so used to that she didn't know if it would ever go away. Her daughter-in-law Sage gave her a tighter than normal hug, kissed both of her cheeks and told her that when she was ready and it was raining, she would walk with her, barefoot, to help Frannie cleanse her aura and reconnect her with the Earth. Frannie nodded, smiled and watched as the family of four walked to their home that was only a block away. Gianna and Bobby had been the first to leave so the house was left to Frannie, Dominic, and Derrick. The couple usually stayed at Frannie's house when they were in town and she assumed that this visit would be no different.

"Ma, we can get a hotel room if you weren't prepared for us. It's really not a big deal, I promise. I know this was a surprise so please don't feel like you have to let us stay." Derrick had their bags by the front door, ready to leave if necessary. Frannie enjoyed Derrick a lot and always had felt comfortable around him. A few other members in their extended family had not been happy when they met Dominic's boyfriend but in Frannie's mind, love was love. If you could find it, you held onto it, no matter what shape or color it came in.

"Absolutely not, you stay here. It's really no problem. This house gets kind of lonely now so it's a very nice change to have someone here with me." Frannie smiled at the both of them, truly wanting them to stay to help fill the void in the big empty house, even if it was only for a few nights. Derrick smiled back at her while picking up the bags, heading to the room he knew well. Dominic followed his Mom back into the kitchen, helping her clean up the dishes and put away the leftovers. It was a long while before either of them talked but it was Dominic who broke the silence.

"I know its dad's birthday and it's hard when he isn't here with us, but I know this is what he would want us to do. He'd want the family together; he'd want all the laughter and the stories. He was the one that told them the most, even the roof one." They both gave a small laugh. Frannie leaned against the counter, watching her middle son talk. "It's different, Mom, I know." Dominic looked down as he continued, "Sometimes I wish I could be here more, visit him more, see the rest of the family more, and we've been toying with the idea of moving back. Derrick can find a job anywhere and I've been thinking of a career change." Frannie didn't know what to say so she waited to see if he would say more but after the silence went on too long, she crossed the kitchen, took her son's hands and looked him in the eyes.

"I don't ever want you to change your life for us. Stay in New York if that's what you want. Come home if you want to. It's your decision. Please don't feel like you need to be home with us. We're fine…I'm fine, I promise. You're right, this is hard, but my heart would break even more to know that you based your decision on me. I want you to be you, Dominic. I want you to be successful and happy. I don't want you to regret anything you've done in your life." She pulled him into a hug as she saw the tears sliding down his cheeks. "You are your own person and I will always, always love you for that. So will your father." Dominic couldn't hold back anymore, he wrapped his arms around his Mom and let out a sob.

"I should be here, Mom. I should be here for everyone. I can't support anyone when I'm not here…I can't be the brother I need to be when I'm 600 miles away." Frannie felt her heart break all over again for her child. The child that always had a tough time expressing his emotions was here, clinging to her in the middle of the kitchen and letting it all out. All she could do was hold him tight, smooth his hair with her hand and give Derrick, who had just walked into the kitchen, the same sad smile that she's had all night. Without missing a beat, he walked over and wrapped his arms around both of them. The three of them stood in the kitchen for a long time, Frannie wishing she could take all the pain away from all of her children.

When Dominic dried his face, he looked between Frannie and Derrick "I think maybe it's time for bed." Both of them nodded and Derrick walked away with Dominic, looking back over his shoulder.

"Do you need any help, Ma? I can come back after he's in bed?"

"No, thanks, I got it. Get some sleep, traveling is exhausting. If I'm not here when you get up…well, you know where everything is." With that, they disappeared and Frannie slumped against the fridge. She didn't know how much longer she could be the rock. The whole time she consoled Dominic, all she wanted to do was break down with him. All she wanted to do all the time is break down. She felt weak and scared for her kids. Who would hold them together if she lost it? She walked to the stairs to see if she could hear anything and when she didn't, Frannie walked out onto the back porch, looking over at the spot in the grass where Hector laid two years earlier. She looked at the patio chair that he had dubbed his throne to his grandkids before sitting down in it, feeling the warm summer air wrap around her like she wished her husband's arms could.

When Frannie was sure no one could hear her, the sobs came. Sobs that were for her children that lost their father, for her grandkids who lost their hero and finally for herself, who lost not only her husband but her best friend, her lover and the one person that knew her inside and out. After months of pushing aside the anxiety and worry she had about Hector, she finally let it fill her. She let herself feel what she's been avoiding and she accepted it. Frannie's life had changed and nothing she did would ever make it go back to what it was. This was her life now. Sitting on the back porch, in Hector's chair, remembering him how he used to be, instead of how he was now.

Chapter 5

Paul sat at this desk, looking over the month end reports that he just generated when there was a knock at the door and Frank McMullen poked his head, "Got a minute?"

"Of course, what's up, Frank?"

Frank walked in slowly, giving Paul the indication that something was wrong. Frank wasn't the best employee but he also wasn't the worst. He wasn't someone that Paul had really gotten to know and honestly, the only reason he'd ever had to talk to him was after Hector's accident. Paul thought back to the sound of the parts falling off the racks, the metallic clangs and screams.

"I just...I have to talk to you...about...about Hector."

This stopped Paul's thoughts instantly and brought his attention back to the man sitting across from him, dressed in a holey zip-up hoodie and dingy blue jeans. He knew he didn't want to be talking to Frank about the accident without a lawyer, he didn't feel comfortable but the tension in the air was thick enough to cut and Paul nodded his head.

"I, eh, this is hard..." Frank stumbled over his words, his voice shaky and cracking as he tried to summon the courage to tell Paul what he's been wanting to for almost two years. He fidgeted with his fingers, picking at the cuticle and eventually watching the blood bead up along his nail. He looked up at Paul then back down. "Um, so this is about the case. I know we shouldn't be talking but...I have to tell you something. I have to get this out. I can't keep doing this..."

"Doing what?" Paul cut him off, growing equally frustrated and curious.

"Living like this. I feel so guilty. I...I can't live like this anymore...I'm not like...suicidal or anything...I think...I mean, I don't want to keep living like this but I don't want to die, I just want you to know the truth." Frank rambled on, not making much sense to Paul. Paul could tell he shouldn't push Frank right now so he just encouraged him to continue.

"Frank, what is it? How can I help?"

"I don't actually know if you can but...remember the drug test, the one that came back saying I had opioids in my system...? And the lawyer said it was a misread, that the machines weren't calibrated correctly and that my sample was mishandled? Well...that's not actually true. Paul...I wanted to tell you. I wanted to be honest, I was just so scared." Frank's eyes started filling with tears.

"Frank...what are you saying?" Paul's head started swimming; he couldn't believe what he was hearing. For two years Paul thought this was a freak accident, he thought the forklift brake system malfunctioned when it hit the racking, sending the parts falling onto Hector. The reason he thought this was because that was the official story from the lawyer and in all the corporate reports. Paul started to realize that this whole time he had been lied to and the guilt that started spreading through his body was unlike anything he had ever felt. He thought of Frannie and Hector, of their kids and grandkids. He had been in on the lie against his friend's family without even knowing it.

"My friend had told me that I should take something, a pain killer or muscle relaxer, I can't really remember... I know it's wrong to take his stuff but man, my back hurt so badly so I took it anyway. I don't know anything about pills or what it would do but my buddy said it would make me feel better and it totally did, just...maybe a little too much." Frank went back to looking at his calloused fingers, watching a trickle of blood starting to run down, a glimpse of vulnerability underneath his hard exterior.

"The next morning when I woke up, I still felt like, I don't know, dizzy and tired, like I hadn't actually slept in forever or had a bad hangover. I know I probably shouldn't have come into work but I had already taken a bunch of days off for my back and I knew I couldn't take any more time. I just kept my head down, didn't talk to nobody. I didn't want anyone to actually see that I was messed up. I mean, no one really ever bugs me anyway. I don't think anyone even noticed. I thought I was going to get through the day no problem but then Arty asked me to move a couple things. I started to panic though, man. I felt like I was swimming and I knew I shouldn't have gotten on the forklift and I thought about telling him that I was sick and had to go home but like I already said, I didn't think I had any more time on the books."

Watching Frank wipe the blood from his finger on to his jeans Paul noticed the other brown spots, an indication that this was Frank's nervous habit. Frank started shaking his head, becoming more upset with every breath. "I was fine for a long time, I kept my eyes forward and paid attention but you know when you're in a car and you start falling asleep because of the shaking? It was kind of like that and before I knew it, I heard this loud scraping sound. I saw that rack start to tip and Paul, I ain't any kind of person that goes to church but I prayed so hard. I prayed to God or Allah or anyone that would listen that the rack would stand back up but it didn't."

Frank took a deep breath to steady his nerves, "The rack went over, the parts starting falling off and then it hit the other one. I heard all those guys start yelling but I had no idea what they were saying. It was as if I had my headphones in. All I heard was my heart, just pounding in my head and it felt like everything was in slow motion. I swear it felt like someone took over my body. I couldn't see, I couldn't breathe. I just jumped off the forklift and ran to the pile. I hoped so hard that all I saw was a pile of parts but when I got around the racks, I saw Hector just lying there. He looked dead; he didn't look like he was breathing. I should have called 9-1-1 but when everyone started coming around us, a few of them were already on the phone. I guess I just assumed they were calling for me."

Paul tried to keep his breath regular, his focus on the man that was spilling his truth out in front of him but he found it hard to separate himself from the situation.

"I just started pulling stuff off of him. I knew I shouldn't move his body but I wanted it to be clear for the guys to help him. I didn't want to waste any time but you know, those parts are so heavy but a couple of guys jumped in to help me. I kept yelling at them to not touch Hector, that he could have some sort of serious injury. Man, it felt like forever before I heard the sirens. I don't even remember who it was that took me away; I just remember that someone grabbed my arm to get me out of the way of the guys. I had no idea if Hector was even still alive; those parts are huge and heavy."

Paul could feel the dread of that day prickling over his skin while he listened to Frank's story. He was a mixture of livid and scared. He didn't know what to do, he felt like he couldn't breathe. Why was Frank telling him this now? Two years after the accident and right before the trial. "Frank…what was your goal by telling me this? What are you doing?"

"I just…had to tell you. I'm sorry I didn't before. I'm sorry it's taken me this long." Frank was sobbing at this point, the regret written all over his face. "It wasn't my idea to lie, I promise. I didn't want to get in trouble but I never meant to hurt anyone. And now Hector is still…like he is and I caused that, I made that happen. I can't take it anymore. I just had to tell someone."

Paul nodded his head, still trying to calm his breathing and asked Frank, "Is there anything else you need to tell me?" Frank just shook his head, wiping his nose on the sleeve of his jacket. "Okay, please, take the rest of the day and go home."

"Okay. I'm so sorry. Please, don't tell anyone else...please. I know I shouldn't have done it, I know I shouldn't..."

"Just go, Frank. Please." Paul put his hand up, wanting him to stop. He needed time to process this information; he needed to figure out what he should do. When Frank shut the door, Paul put his head down on his desk and closed his eyes. If he didn't know about this, how did anyone else? This was going to go from a workplace accident case to a criminal case if this got out. The flip side to that was that Paul would be part of this lie and there was no way he wanted to do that to his friends. He couldn't just sit here anymore, Paul had to go. He let the other supervisor know that he was going home early. Getting into his car, he knew that he wasn't going home. It had been a long time since he had visited Hector and today seemed like as good of a day as any.

He pulled up to Hope Covenant, the facility that Hector had been in for a while, but that Paul had only been to once, and parked in a spot facing the door. It was a nice enough building and the staff was friendly, but the anxiety that washed over him as he started towards the flowers flanking the doors almost made him turn around. He forced himself out of his car, willing his legs to carry him across the parking lot and through the automatic doors. He felt as if he were floating across the ground as if he were outside of his own body. He had to ask the front desk which room Hector was in, feeling like the worst friend in the world. Making his way up the stairs, needing to feel the blood pumping in his body, he prepared himself mentally to see his old friend.

"Hello, Nurse! I am ready for my sponge bath!"

Hector had to do something to keep himself entertained all day, even if it was joking with himself over something that actually happened regularly and was not at all sexual. He heard the footsteps coming into the room and instantly recognized the hesitance in them. This was someone new, not his family and not a nurse. He could feel the tension in the air and the uncertainty in the presence.

Paul reached Hector's side, looking down at the fragile body that couldn't possibly have been his friend that used to be so full of life. He looked so different than he did the last time Paul had seen him and Paul wondered how he could possibly get any worse. At first, Paul didn't speak. He didn't know what to say, only that he wanted to physically see Hector. He remembered that the nurses had told him last time to talk to Hector; it was a technique that they thought could help bring him out of his coma. Paul cleared his throat and spoke, "Hey man, it's me."

"Paul? Paul...where have you been?"

Hector long ago gave up on their friendship, angry that Paul had abandoned him during the worse part of his life.

"I, eh, I know I haven't been around a lot lately, but I think about you constantly. I think about Frannie and everything she's doing for you. I think about your kids…"

Hector was thoughtless, he was shocked that Paul was here and he was wondering why. Frannie had talked about the court case and the upcoming trial date so he wondered if this had anything to do with that. Whatever it was, Hector was glad to have his old friend there, he couldn't remember the last time that Paul had come to visit but he could tell there was something wrong.

"Hector, I eh, I didn't mean to be away for so long, I just…I don't really know what to say or even really how to say it. The trial day is coming up and I just…got some really…" Paul took a deep breath and pulled a chair over to the side of Hector's bed, "some really mind-blowing information about it. I don't even really know what to do, man."

"Paul...what are you talking about, what kind of information...? What's going on?"

Hector tried to move anything, to let Paul know that he was there and listening but nothing moved, not even a twitch.

"I don't know if I should go to the lawyer but I think Frank said it was the lawyer that started covering it all up..."

"Covering what up? Paul, covering what up? What does Frank have anything to do with this? Frank who?"

"I think I need to tell Frannie...I can't lie to you guys anymore, even if I didn't know I was lying..."

"Frannie doesn't know? Doesn't know what? Paul...my accident...that's what it was, an accident. What

could be so mind-blowing about it? Did someone do it on purpose?"

"Frank feels so bad, I can tell he feels bad but he lied…for almost two years Hector, he lied to everyone and so did the lawyer. I'm so mad; they knew that if it came out that he was high that this case wouldn't have a leg to stand on!"

"He was…high? Frank…that jackass from the lunchroom? He's the one that did this? He's the one that caused this? And he was high?! Paul, you have to tell someone! You cannot keep this a secret! You have to tell Frannie!"

Hector knew that Paul couldn't hear him, he knew that he couldn't do anything about this but Frannie had to know, she had to tell her lawyer about it. If Paul didn't tell her, who would? The monitors hooked up to Hector retained their same rhythmic beeping but Hector could feel something happening.

He felt as if an elephant had sat on his chest. The machines helping him breathe weren't going deep enough like they were fighting against Hector's natural breathing and he felt as if he would pass out, if he weren't already in a coma.

Paul sat back in his chair, bouncing his leg and running his hand through his hair, completely oblivious of the distress his best friend was going through. Not a single muscle twitched, nothing new came on the monitors and Hector appeared to be peacefully sleeping.

"Paul, please...please get someone. I...I think I'm actually dying now...I think..."

Hector continued to struggle, internally, until all of a sudden, after only about 30 seconds, he could breathe a little easier and the weight on his chest started to lift.

"What was that...? What...why...oh God, I knew something else was wrong. I just...I need someone to know...I feel like I can't take a full breath like this machine is fighting against me. I want to take a deep breath, I want to fill my lungs with air, on my own and this machine won't let me."

"Well man...I guess I've taken up enough of your time...I need to figure this out...I need to do something, I can't just sit on this information...someone needs to know, I just...I don't know what to do..." Paul started to stand but then saw Frannie standing in the door, staring at him with a look of concern on her face.

"Paul...? What are you doing here?" She crossed the room and gave him a hug. "What were you just talking about...with Hector? What information...?"

Paul thought for a moment, this was his chance to tell Frannie but looking down at her, he knew he couldn't bring himself to do it. "Oh, just work stuff. Hector used to help me make key decisions and I'm struggling with this one so I wanted to get his opinion." He hoped he had been convincing

71

enough. He hated lying to Frannie but he also didn't want to upset her right now. The trial was less than a week away, he had a few days to decide on what he was going to do but right now, he was leaving. "I'm sorry, I have to get back to work but I'll come by and see you soon, okay?"

"Okay. You sure it's nothing I can help with? Maybe I'd know how Hector would handle it?"

"Nope, I got this one. Thanks, Fran." With that, Paul patted her shoulder and walked out of the room, letting his breath escape his lungs. He leaned on the wall for a minute, his vision blurred from tears that he desperately wanted to keep to himself then rushed out of the building.

Hector's room was in the front of the building, so when Frannie looked out the window, down to the parking lot, she saw Paul walking to his car. She saw him get into the driver's seat and push his head into the steering wheel, hitting it a couple times with his hands. She didn't know what to think about this behavior from him, someone who usually has it all together but she also didn't think it was odd. A friend coming to see another friend who has been in a coma is a stressful situation so Frannie let it go from her mind. She walked over to Hector and smiled down at him.

"Hi there, handsome. Work was…challenging today. We had a new student start and she just…she has a hard time with life." Hector was thankful that Frannie continued to come to see him every day after work. He knew that working with kids that have behavior issues was a lot to mentally handle and coming to talk to your husband that couldn't talk back didn't help with the stress. He knew that Frannie loved helping children and that she loved him too but he wouldn't be surprised if one day coming to visit him became too much.

"She just needs a little extra attention, she's severely autistic and lashes out but I totally get it. I couldn't imagine being in a world where I knew what I wanted to say but I just couldn't get it out, where I couldn't let people know what I was trying to say. I feel so awful for them all. Think about it. She's brand new to the school, it's a new place where people don't understand how she communicates and she can't comprehend what we're trying to tell her."

"Oh Frannie, I know exactly how that is…"

"I just wish I could get into her head, to see what she's thinking and how she's thinking. I wish I could understand her better…" Frannie sat in the chair that Paul had been in only a few minutes before. She rubbed her fingertips gently across Hector's temple, "I wish I could get into your head too. I wish I knew if you were in pain or if you were sad…I wish I knew what I could do to help you, too." Frannie planted a kiss where her fingers had been and looked over at the door as it opened and Patty walked in.

"Hey Frannie, still the same. Nothing new." She walked over to the sink, washed her hands then walked over to Hector. She patted his arm and recorded some information from the monitors before turning to Frannie. "Thank you for coming to see him every day. I know he's your husband but you'd be surprised how many people stop coming. How many people are here, that have no visitors, ever. Hector is a very lucky man, considering the circumstances."

"Yes, Frannie…Thank you."

She moved around the room like it was muscle memory, talking over her shoulder now, "There is something that concerns me a little bit. I don't know how much weight it carries and really, I probably shouldn't say anything to you about it without the doctors. He's rapidly losing more weight and I can't figure out why. He's on the same nutrition he's been on and it's not like he's exercising." Patty always tried to throw a small joke in there and Frannie smiled, humoring her.

"Ha-Ha. She's just so funny."

Hector mentally rolled his eyes, not thinking her jokes were funny at all.

"So, he's losing weight? I know he looks skinny but…I guess with the blankets and machines and stuff, I don't see a change. Does that make me awful? That I don't see a change…should I?" Frannie looked Hector up and down, trying to find any sign of weight loss but she wasn't seeing it. She looked at Patty, trying to see if this was another one of her jokes.

"Fran! You will never be awful! I'm fine…I think."

Hector still felt like he was having trouble breathing but the elephant that was on his chest had relocated to some other poor schmuck.

"Well, I guess when I say rapidly, I mean in medical terms. You won't be able to see it but with us, a couple ounces for someone that is on a steady diet and not moving, is not really a concern, just something we're going to watch but the doctor isn't as concerned as I am." She walked over and put her hand on Hector's arm.

"So she shouldn't be concerned? Patty? Then why even say anything?! Frannie, ugh, I wish you could ignore her. She loves the gossip and doesn't really know when to turn it off, believe me. She's told me some wild things!"

"So should I not be concerned? It's not a big deal?" Frannie looked up at Patty from the chair. She knew that Patty was a great nurse and that she took really good care of Hector but sometimes she didn't follow her line of thinking.

"Nope. I just want to let you know that we were going to keep an eye on it. Nothing you need to worry about. He's still okay, still not worse. Remember, no news is good news in this case."

Hector wanted to throw up, he was so sick of hearing that phrase and he knew that Frannie was too. He wished he could see the look on her face right now, he could picture it.

A tight smile, not wanting to offend the other person, her eyes opened wide and her eyebrows high on her forehead. It's a look that Hector has seen many times, one that he knows is Frannie trying her best to not explode. He knew his wife well because the way she was tightening her grip on his arm proved that the look is one that followed Patty as she walked out of the room. As soon as the door was closed, Frannie relaxed.

"Hector, I swear…if someone says that again, I'm going to lose my mind. I want news, good news. I hate no news. "

"I know darling, I wish I could lose my mind with you. We could go on such great adventures together in our imaginations. You wouldn't believe what I can come up with now."

Hector felt the weight of Frannie's head on his shoulder and the tickle of her hair on his cheek. These were

Moments he cherished, even if they only lasted a few minutes and the pressure of her head hurt his body, he still wouldn't trade it for anything except maybe a real life.

"I've got to go, baby. I wish I could stay longer but I told Gianna I'd watch Bobby tonight. She has a date. I just hope it goes well. I know she's doing fine alone, but I would love to see her with someone that could take care of her and Bobby. Someone that is good for them. I'll let you know how it goes tomorrow." Frannie kissed his cheek, leaving her soft lips against it for a second longer. Hector heard her soft footsteps leaving the room and was desperate to take in every breath he could that had her perfume mingled with oxygen. Frannie coming to visit him was the highlight of his day. When she walked out it left him feeling even emptier than he already did. He was able to slide back into the depressive thoughts that just didn't seem to want to go away without any interruptions. That never leads to anything good. Hector was alone again, physically and mentally. He was the only one that knew his body was shutting down and he had no one to tell.

Chapter 6

Summer storms were ones that Hector always enjoyed. He loved feeling the warmth of the air but the coolness of each raindrop on his skin. The electricity in the air flowing through everything it touched. Frannie hated them, not because she was scared but because Hector always ran out in them. Behind him, their children. When the news was telling everyone to get inside and take shelter, the Plata family was out in it. Hector and the three kids running around in the rain and Frannie on the front porch, yelling for them to all come inside. This had happened every time a big storm came which was pretty frequent in Southeast Michigan. The storm outside Hector's window sounded like the perfect one. He heard the rain tapping against the glass and the branches of the tree occasionally interrupting their song. He heard and felt the rumble of the thunder in his chest and could see the flashes of lights through the skin on his eyelids. The hair on his arms prickled after an exceptionally loud roar of thunder. The clouds were showing off, as Hector's dad used to tell him. It was through storms like this that Hector felt as if he could relax a little in his new life. He could focus on the rain as it wrote a beautiful melody, the wind and the thunder adding in the bass and percussion sections. Preventing his thoughts from getting increasingly dark, like the clouds outside.

He missed the moments with his children, running in the warm sprinkles and hearing their laughter carried on the wind. There was only one time that Frannie actually joined them in their rain dance and it was against her will. Hector ran up to the porch, faking that he was getting ready to come inside when he scooped Frannie up over his shoulder. Running back out into the rain, his plan was to set her on the ground with the kids. Chasing her through the raindrops but like life, plans don't always work out. Instead of running out into the yard, Hector ran a few feet before he hit a flooded part of their front lawn, slipped in the mud and fell backward. Frannie falling on top of him. Hector, hesitant to look at his wife, sat up and looked over at Frannie. She was covered in mud and to his relief, laughing. The children, all young at the time, less than 10 years old, ran over to them, jumping onto their parents. All five of them were now covered in mud, sitting in the grass during a warm summer storm.

Hector loved his memories because they were all he had left. He couldn't talk to his family anymore; he couldn't touch them or hold them. He couldn't even look at them. All he could do was remember what they looked like, what they were like outside of a hospital room and hold on to those memories for as long as he could. It had been two years since he had seen any of his children or his wife. He imagined what they looked like now, what his grandkids were growing up to look like. He had only seen Buzz as a newborn but now he was two. He was walking and babbling and had the cutest little voice. Hector had no way of knowing what he actually looked like, which was a thought he tried to stay away from. He wasn't sure if he would even recognize his grandkids or maybe even his kids if he were ever able to open his eyes again.

It was late at night, or Hector thought it was. He didn't hear anything in the hallway and his nurse hadn't come in a long while. The last one quickly running through the checklist of things to do while talking with someone else. Patty was on vacation, she'd told him she was leaving for a family trip to Traverse City a few days ago. She assured him that he would be in great hands and while he wanted to believe her, he hadn't had a nurse check on him very often and he was feeling a little off. He wasn't entirely sure how but he knew that something was wrong, something other than his chest.

The pain in Hector's chest had not fully gone away since Paul had been there to visit him and his breathing continued to feel labored. Still, the monitors didn't pick anything up, they kept on with their beeping, and joining the clock in their constant reminders that life was passing him by. He wasn't sure why the monitors weren't picking up these episodes and why no one had known he was in pain and always worrying about if the next one will kill him.

Hector started feeling as if he were in the summer storm instead of trying to relax to the sound of it. It started off slow, a little gurgle here and there, the feeling of needing to clear his throat but now he felt as if he were trapped underwater with no air. The natural reaction to the wet feeling had been to swallow but along with every other muscle in his body his throat didn't want to hook up to his brain to do what he needed it to. Hector was starting to get desperate and as much as he knew that panicking wouldn't help him; his body was doing what it wanted. He willed his arms to move, his head to turn and his throat to swallow. He focused on each muscle in his neck individually, wanting them to do anything. He wanted the alarms on his monitors to go off, the nurse to walk in or for the tree to crash into the room, anything to get someone there to help him breathe. The gurgling of his own throat reached his ears, hearing the sound and knowing it was his body making it made Hector sick. All he could do was lie there, listening to his throat, knowing he was about to die if he didn't get help.

He knew that the nurse that had come into the room before but Hector had been so focused on the storm that it didn't occur to him that she would have missed anything. Especially something this important. Patty was very good at making sure Hector was comfortable and that included suctioning out the saliva that pools in the back of Hector's throat so it was routine for him to depend on her to live, along with the machines. He had long gotten over the embarrassment of having someone do everything but think for him and accepted that Patty and the other nurses were going to see, hear and have to clean much more than he would have liked them to.

It had not been even a full minute but Hector felt as if it had been a lifetime when he heard the rumble of the cleaning cart. He wanted to call out to them, to yell that he needed help but he couldn't. He prayed that they were going to come into his room first. Over the gurgling that was coming from his throat he heard the cart stop, he heard footsteps walking past his room, stop then turn around. Hector was filled with relief when he heard the hinge on the door move and a female voice yelling to someone else, "Hey, this guy is making a weird noise, go get a nurse." He heard her walk over to him and felt as she put her hand on his arm, pushing a bit. "Are you all right? Sir? Are you okay?"

Hector wanted to shake his head, to get her to hurry someone along but all he could do was lay there, not being able to breathe, not being able to let anyone know he was slowly fading. Finally, the machine next to him started beeping, alarms going off as his heart slowed down. When he thought it was too late a team of people came rushing into his room, someone coming to his side, taking a moment to assess the situation then leaping into action. Hector heard yelling, he heard someone giving orders to the other people in the room. He willed them to work faster, his mind feeling as if he were falling asleep. Just as he was slipping, he felt relief, he felt the suction in his throat; he felt the pool of saliva disappear and finally he felt like he could breathe. Slowly the machines started to quiet and people started to clear the room. The conversation that stood out was between two women, a conversation that he would resent for the rest of his days.

"What happened?"

"I don't know, I guess I forgot to suction him out during last rounds but…he wasn't making that noise, he didn't seem to need it." Hector could hear the woman whispering next to him and judging from the quieting of footsteps he knew the rest of the room was emptying out.

"He won't always make that noise, only when he's choking. You always have to do it, always. It's not an option"

"Okay, okay. I get it." There was a pause in the conversation, then some hesitance. "Would it really be such a bad thing though? I know his family would be sad but like, maybe his wife would be a little relieved to not have to come here every day. He just lays there…taking up her money, her time. I don't know how she does it every day. I probably would have already pulled the plug." Hector heard the two women giggle as they walked out of the room.

"That's so mean to say but yeah, I probably would have too. It'll be sad but she'll get over it. He's been gone for a long time."

Even though Hector was mad, he knew they were right. He knew that he was just a source of pain and headache for his family. He wished they knew how many times he'd hoped to die. He wished that he had the ability to move on. He knew his family would be sad but he also knew that eventually, they would get over it. They would move on with their lives. Their husband, dad, and grandpa just a fond memory they can think back on when feeling nostalgic during the holidays. Right now, Hector wished no one would have found him and he would have drowned, giving his family the last bit of closure that they need to move on.

Hector tried to pay attention to the storm. To refocus on the raindrops, to feel the roar of the thunder but all he kept wondering if Frannie felt the way the nurses did. If she secretly wished Hector would die so she could move on with her life instead of wasting it talking to a man that would never talk back. The night went on like any other uneventful night and while Hector typically followed a usual sleep-wake routine, tonight he stayed awake, thinking about his life and what was left of it.

Frannie lay awake that night, listening to the storm as it rolled through her neighborhood, only getting a few hours of restless sleep. She loved working, especially with the children she worked with, but the thought of getting out of bed on Monday morning was tough. She didn't know if it was the storm that had kept her awake or if it was the thought of the upcoming court case. She was filled with dread thinking about hearing all of the details of what happened the day of Hector's accident. Ironically, the anniversary was only a few days after the trial. Sliding her feet into a pair of slippers Hector had bought for her one Christmas, she headed downstairs, far ahead of her typical morning routine. Staying in bed didn't seem like much of an option anymore so Frannie got a head start. She made an actual breakfast of eggs and toast instead of her normal cup of coffee. Even though she was exhausted, she wanted to turn her attitude around; she wanted today to be a good day. The new little girl that Frannie was shadowing, Amelia, deserved Frannie at her best and that's what she wanted to give her, her full focus, attention, and devotion.

Walking into Hope Covenant, Frannie couldn't wait to tell Hector about the breakthrough she'd had at work. Amelia had not only participated in the daily activities but she seemed to have made a friend today, which was something her parents and Frannie were concerned about. Frannie felt good and she knew that there would have been no way today would have been a success if she let the negativity seep into her mind. Frannie smiled at everyone she passed in the hallway up to Hector's room and when she walked in, Patty was there.

"Well, hi! How was your vacation? You look tan; spend a lot of time at the beach?" Frannie said while putting her bags down by the window.

"Oh great, ask her so I have to listen to this story again. She's already told me and the other nurse that stopped in here."

"Yes, I sure did. It was wonderful." Patty stopped what she was doing and looked right at Frannie. "I'm sorry to hear about what happened to Hector. That must have been very scary. I can only apologize to you, I feel really bad that happened while I was away. There's no way it would have happened if I was here." Frannie froze, not knowing what Patty was talking about.

Hector could tell by Frannie's silence that she had no idea what Patty was talking about.

"I knew no one told you, Fran. I knew if you knew you would have been here hours ago."

"What do you mean? What happened to him...?" Frannie watched as Patty's face fell and her eyes went wide.

"Last night...when he stopped breathing...did no one tell you? Frannie, please tell me someone called you." The words hung in the air in front of her.

"Of course they didn't call her. They don't actually care about any of us. You think they'd make sure to call her when they couldn't even do the job right in the first place?"

"He stopped breathing? No, no one called me. Patty, what are you talking about? He stopped breathing?" Frannie felt herself starting to panic. She looked down, closed her eyes and took a few deep breaths. She had no idea that anything had happened and she couldn't believe that she wasn't called about it. She was about to walk out of the room when Patty moved in front of her, shutting the door.

"Frannie, I know you're upset. Please, sit down. I'll tell you what I know. Then you can go talk to the supervisor. You just have to calm down first." Frannie looked at Patty then nodded, going back to Hector's side, looking down at him. Nothing seemed out of place and if Patty hadn't mentioned the incident, she would have never known it happened by simply looking at Hector.

"What I was told was that someone didn't suction him out, they caught it in time but he did stop breathing. I know it sounds scary but he's okay now, and it's being talked about throughout the facility so it shouldn't happen again. You are absolutely allowed to be mad and you should be, just please think before you talk to anyone." Frannie could only nod, trying to process the information. She was mad. Very mad. She wanted to talk to someone about it, about why she wasn't contacted and about why a routine procedure was missed but she knew Patty was right. She would give it some time. Her mother used to tell her to take 24 hours before reacting so she had plenty of time to evaluate the situation. Right now she was just thankful that Hector was okay.

"My love, I wish I could have told you. You know I would have let you know if I could."

Hector hated hearing his wife this mad and upset especially because of him.

Patty walked around the bed, putting her hand on Frannie's arm with a small smile. "Be mad, Frannie, just be smart." She touched Hector's arm then walked out of the room, leaving Frannie and Hector alone.

"Oh Hector, I'm so sorry, I wish I would have known. I would have been here for you. I hate that this happened to you. I'm sure it was scary…" She trailed off, tears welling up in her eyes at the thought that Hector could have actually been gone. These thoughts were overriding the news from work that Frannie had been so excited to tell him. She knew that Hector couldn't talk back to her but there was comfort in knowing that there was a slight chance that he could hear her and if that was the case, she would come back, day after day, to be by her husband.

Frannie knew it was wrong but she didn't tell her children about the incident. She kept it to herself until she could rationally make a decision on what to do. She knew she had to talk to someone at Hope Covenant but she didn't know where to go from there. For the time being, she would sleep on it and make her decision in the morning. A whirlwind of a day, emotions from every corner, ended just like it began, with Frannie lying wide awake in her bed, thinking of Hector.

After another restless night of sleep, Frannie had decided that she would talk to the supervisor and request that the nurse that forgot the procedure not be assigned to Hector. She knew it was a long shot and hoped that the nurse had been talked to and properly disciplined. Frannie had a plan, she knew she would be strong and she knew that she would have to stand up for her husband since he couldn't be his own advocate. After work, Frannie was going to go straight to the supervisor and let her know everything she thought about the situation, she wouldn't back down. The confident streak followed her through the morning drive and came to a screeching halt right as she pulled into the school's parking lot. That's when her cell phone rang and "Hope Covenant Facility" flashed across the screen. Her heart sank deep into her stomach, knowing that calls don't come unless something is wrong.

"Hello?"

"Hi, Mrs. Plata? This is Christine from Hope Covenant." There was a hint of hesitation coming through the phone and Frannie wanted to scream at the woman and beat on her steering wheel, asking her why she didn't call her two nights ago.

"There's been...eh, there's been an incident with Hector and we need you to come see us, please?"

"I know about the suction, I found out yesterday. You're a little late calling me about this." Frannie usually wasn't so harsh, it must have been the lack of sleep and the stress mixing together to give her this new attitude.

"No, Mrs. Plata, I apologize for not calling you about that, this is...something new. We just need you to come here, please? We need you to see this." Frannie started shaking. Something new. What could be new? Why couldn't she tell her over the phone?

"Oh...is everything okay? I'm on my way, is he okay?"

"He's fine; he's...actually more than fine."

Frannie didn't know what to think as she hung up the phone and called her boss, letting her know that there was an emergency and she wouldn't be in today. At that moment Frannie thanked God that she had an understanding workplace, one that knew her situation and didn't give her any trouble when she needed to leave. She felt bad for abandoning the children but right now her husband was her priority and she needed to get to him.

Running past the front desk, the nurses, patients and families straight up to Hector's room, she was conflicted on how to feel. The caller sounded distant but she had said Hector was more than fine. Frannie just needed to know what was going on, as soon as possible. She was relieved to see Patty's familiar face in the room when she opened the door. She also saw who she assumed was Christine, a young, red-haired woman wearing a white coat. She must be new, Frannie had never seen her before or maybe she was just always preoccupied when she came to visit Hector. Frannie didn't see what was different in the room right away but she could feel and hear a difference. She looked around, then at the two women, both smiling.

"Can someone tell me what's going on? Why did I have to come here now? Is Hector okay?" Frannie was desperate for someone to fill her in.

Patty was the first to speak, "Frannie, look at Hector." Frannie let her eyes fall on her husband, watching him, his chest rising and falling, looking as if he was sleeping and that's when it hit her. Hector wasn't hooked up to a ventilator anymore. Surprise spread across her face as she searched the room for the missing equipment. While Hector was breathing on his own, Frannie felt as if she would need some help. She ran to his side, looking him over, placing her hand gently on his chest, feeling the movement his body was making on its own. She couldn't help herself as tears spilled over and slid down her cheeks. Looking up at Patty, she wiped her eyes with one hand, not removing the other from Hector's chest.

"How did this happen…? I mean, why is it happening? He just started breathing? I don't understand."

It was now Christine's turn to talk. She walked over to Frannie's side, pulling two chairs up so they could sit.

"Okay. Hector is fantastic; he is breathing on his own which is a huge milestone for him. After two years on the ventilator, this is leaps and bounds towards a good outcome."

Frannie was so overwhelmed with happiness that she had a hard time understanding what was going on. She didn't know how they'd figured this out because Hector had been on a ventilator since he had been put into a coma and never came off. The only time it wasn't hooked up was when they had to suction out his throat. Thinking of this brought Frannie back to the day before. She wasn't sure if this had anything to do with the incident but it instantly made her freeze.

"I see that and I'm shocked...I guess I'm just confused, does this have anything to do with the other day? When he started choking?"

Both Patty and Christine looked at each other then back at Frannie, she could tell there was some hesitation when Christine started talking.

"Yes and no. No, this wasn't directly caused by...the incident, but in a way, influenced?" Frannie was confused by the tone in Christine's voice.

"What do you mean "influenced?" Can you please just tell me what's going on?"

"The nurse that was performing the procedure, the suction, well, when you do that you have to disconnect Hector's ventilator and shut the alarm off, otherwise it'll continue to go off because it's not hooked up anymore. When the nurse removed it she was very focused on the procedure so that what happened before didn't happen again and she didn't...well, when she was done she didn't hook it back up and because the alarm was shut off, it didn't alert anyone that it wasn't connected." Frannie felt the blood rising in her veins; she felt the heat in her face. She looked over at Patty, shaking her head.

"So...you're telling me that my husband could have died...AGAIN because someone did something wrong? Again."

Christine nodded and Patty looked away.

"Mrs. Plata, I understand your frustration and believe me, the nurse is going to have disciplinary actions taken against her, but we're trying to focus on the positive, which is that Hector is breathing on his own. That means that his body is getting better, his lungs are working on their own now, that's a huge step forward, it's pretty fantastic."

Frannie knew that Patty wasn't involved but she also trusted the facility to keep Hector alive, not to make mistakes that could kill him. Frannie tried to keep herself calm. She tried to hold in the anger that had been bubbling up but this time she couldn't.

"That is fantastic because now it means I can take him home. He doesn't need this machine anymore? Good! He will be coming home with me so I can take care of him. Maybe we will have less death scares if he's in good hands. Now please, leave so I can have some time with my husband." Frannie turned away from the two women, not wanting to look at them any longer. She instantly regretted speaking to Patty that way but when she turned back, the door was closing.

My love, I am so proud of you for standing up for me, but I have to admit, I am scared to go home. This is a lot of work, taking care of me. I may not be on a ventilator anymore but Frannie; this is too much work for you to do alone...You truly do not need to do this..."

"Oh Hector, I'm so sorry. I can do this. I can take care of you without making these mistakes. Look at you..." Frannie laid her hand back on Hector's chest, very gently as to not cause him any harm, "...you're breathing on your own, Hector. You might actually come back to me." For the first time in two years, Frannie crawled into the bed with Hector. She pulled his arm around her and laid her head on his chest. She was hesitant to put much pressure on him, as he was just a frail version of his old self, but she wanted to feel his chest rise and fall naturally. Being in Hector's arms again gave Frannie a new sense of hope. She could do it. She could take Hector home and she could take care of him, she knew she could. She closed her eyes, tears flowing freely down her face and onto Hector's chest, the emotions a mix of anger at the facility, hope for the future and the fear of failing Hector. At the sound of his heart beating, Frannie was transported back to a happier time, their wedding night. Frannie thought about the love they shared and their dreams for the future. She cried for the wasted arguments and the hours she spent not talking to Hector. She regretted all the times she ignored him or wished he would go away for a while. Right now, all Frannie wanted to do was go back in time and fix all of their mistakes.

"Frannie, I've missed holding you, I've missed touching you." This was all Hector wanted, to be able to hold his girl one more time.

Chapter 7

Frannie finally sat down while waiting for the medical transport company to bring Hector home. After what felt like a tornado of furniture moving and carpet cleaning, Frannie was finally able to breathe. She had transformed her dining room into a new bedroom for Hector and she deep cleaned the rest of her house, trying to get everything as clean as possible. All of her children had come to help her clean and plan for their father's return home. Dominic and Derrick decided to move back to Michigan to help out Frannie, as much as she protested. Dominic said he wanted to be there, in the same house, to help both his father and his mother and she couldn't fight him anymore. As much as she wanted him to stay in New York, explore his life and excel in his career she was grateful for the help it would bring. She didn't want to admit it, but Frannie was starting to second guess her decision.

She finally had a moment to herself. Angelo insisted on being the one to be with his father when he came home and Gianna had gone to the airport with Bobby to pick up Dominic. Derrick was staying in New York for another week, tying up loose ends before moving to Michigan. After Frannie did a few last minute things around the house, she could finally breathe a little easier knowing that Hector was going to be so close to her, right in the home they've shared for the last 3 decades. Her life was about to change, again, and she wondered if she was she ready for it.

She thought about how just a few days ago, she had been all alone in this big house, feeling like the walls were going to close in on her. She felt as if the house might swallow her whole and she even thought about selling it but couldn't bring herself to do it. Her children had grown up in this house; their memories were something Frannie couldn't give away. She couldn't part with the doorframe that had heights from over the years drawn on in little lines with markers. She couldn't stand not seeing the faint blue stain on the wall from where Leaf drew his masterpiece in what Frannie thought was a washable marker but quickly figured out it wasn't. She was ready for this change; she was ready to not be so lonely, even if the person she was excited to be home with wouldn't bring much conversation.

Like the true planner that Frannie was, she set up a schedule that everyone could be on board with. She would continue to work while Dominic stayed home with his dad and when she got home, Dominic and Frannie would share the responsibilities. She even had a long-time neighbor, a retired nurse, who offered to help her anytime she needed it. Everyone connected to Frannie had gathered around her for support and guidance. Her children rallied behind her after she told them about the incidents at the facility and did whatever they could to help bring Hector home.

There was a knock on the door as it opened and Frannie knew that it was Hector and Angelo. She stood up from the loveseat, making her way towards the noise, watching two men roll Hector into the house, just after Angelo. This was not the way she thought Hector would be coming home after his accident, but she tried to tell herself that this was a good move.

"Honey, he's home!" Angelo smiled at his mother, trying to make light of a situation that they both knew was very scary.

"Hey man, I'm supposed to say that! Honey, I'm home!"

Hector's trip had been one that he had been looking forward to and dreading all at the same time. He had been alone in a room for so long that the thought of getting into a vehicle, even if he were strapped to a gurney, made him excited but the thought of going home, to no doctors and just his family to care for him scared him. He knew he would be in great hands, but he also knew that the pain in his chest hadn't gone away and he worried that it would continue to get worse. He also knew that by being home, he was sucking up more of their time, their money and their mental health.

Angelo led the men into the dining room where they transferred Hector into the new bed. Frannie was by his side, her eyes focused on his chest, making sure that the stress of moving hadn't made him take any steps backward. She was incredibly hopeful that Hector would make a recovery, maybe not a full one, but a recovery nonetheless. She smiled at her son when she saw that Hector was successfully in his bed and still breathing on his own. The men hooked up Hectors monitors, his feeding supplies and made sure he was stable before shaking Frannie and Angelo's hand as they walked out.

The two stood outside the dining room, looking in at the most precious man in both of their lives, finally home after his accident. The table in the dining room had been moved to one side of the room and Hector's bed and equipment were on the other side. Angelo put his arm around his mom and gave her a squeeze.

"This is going to work, Mom. He's getting better. He's breathing now and who knows, maybe he'll wake up soon." Angelo said these words to his mother, wanting to believe them but having a hard time. He didn't fully support his father's move, he knew it was risky but he had never seen his mother so angry and he trusted that she knew what she was doing. Angelo wanted his father to be in a facility where doctors were seconds away and nurses were constantly checking on him. That was part of the reason that he had called his brother. He knew Dominic had been debating a move back home and he knew that this would be a way to make sure their father had round-the-clock care. Dominic didn't hesitate and booked his flight home arriving two days later.

Frannie smiled up at her son, feeling bittersweet. She loved that Hector was home but was scared of what it might mean if something were to happen. She moved into the dining room, walking up to Hector and placing a kiss on his forehead, whispering, "Welcome home, handsome. I promise I will do my best." She meant it. Frannie had vowed to be with Hector through sickness and in health and this must have been exactly what they were talking about.

"Darling, it's good to be home. The house smells the same, you must have just cooked something, or maybe you're cooking it now. Either way, it smells the same. I missed this. I missed my home with you, but Frannie, I really want you to reconsider what you're doing."

Hector took in everything around him, the smells and the sounds. The house smelled like a home cooked meal, pot roast with potatoes and carrots and maybe even some rolls. He heard the familiar ticking of the Black Forest Cuckoo clock in the hallway. This ticking didn't make him feel pressured about his life wasting away like the clock in his old room, instead he was reminded of all the years he spent complaining about it during the night. Frannie had insisted on keeping it after her parents got it for their 10-year wedding anniversary even after Hector woke up constantly to all the noise it made. The incessant ticking and tocking along with the cuckoos and chimes that went off every half hour letting you know what time it was had Hector wanting to take a bat to it. There were many times that he had imagined the dark brown walnut buck from the top of the clock lying on the floor, his antlers shattered around him. He imagined the horn that encircled the face of the clock broken into tiny pieces and the pinecone weights shattered across the ground. He so badly wanted to destroy this clock but the love for his wife overpowered his hate for the timepiece. Frannie said it made the house feel like a home, which is why Hector felt so calm and relaxed now.

She put her hand on Hector's chest, needing the physical reassurance that this was truly happening before turning to Angelo. "Thank you for being with him and for helping me so much. Gianna should be here soon. She has Bobby and Dominic with her. I have a roast in the oven if you want to stay for dinner. Call Sage, see if she'll bring the boys over. We can have our first meal as a full family since the accident."

"Of course I'll call her, Mom. She and the boys can walk over in a few." Angelo walked out of the room, pulling his cell phone out of his back pocket.

Frannie turned back to Hector, forcing herself to be strong and to believe in herself because if she didn't, how could anyone else? She kissed him again, this time on his lips, something she didn't do very often. Somehow kissing Hector almost felt wrong. She didn't know if it was because he couldn't kiss her back or if it was something else. She thought about how warm his lips were but also how chapped. She mentally added that to the list of things she wanted to do for Hector: Apply ChapStick. Specifically, cherry chapstick because for as long as she's known Hector, that had been one of the staples in his pocket.

After working in the kitchen for a while, making sure dinner was still on track, Frannie heard the front door open and close, little feet running towards her and Bobby yelling, "Grandma! Uncle Dominic is here! It's a surprise! You can't tell Grampa. I'm gonna tell him!"

Frannie acted surprised and put her finger to her mouth, "You gotta be quiet about it then, Grampa is right in the dining room, he might hear you! Go ahead; go tell him before he hears Uncle Dominic."

Bobby ran off towards the dining room, turning the corner and leaning on Hector's bed, getting close to his ear. Hector could feel his warm breath on the side of his face and smell the fruity piece of candy he had recently eaten. Bobby did his best to whisper but only being 6 years old, it was more of a hushed yell, "Grampa, Uncle Dominic is here to surprise you! Mommy and I just picked him up from the airport. He got to ride on one of those huge big planes. He told me he was going to stay for a long time, isn't that awesome?" His voice got louder as his secret went on.

Hector loved when Bobby was around, he was always so excited to see his grampa and always willing to talk to him.

"Uncle Dominic is here? Oh man, I had no idea he was going to be here. It is totally awesome, buddy."

Even though Bobby couldn't hear him, Hector couldn't help but play along.

Hector enjoyed being home, he loved hearing all his grandsons around him and he loved feeling like part of the family. He felt involved even though he couldn't interact, he was physically there and his family included him. He loved smelling the food Frannie cooked and his stomach growled, he wished he were able to eat something solid. He loved hearing the dinnertime conversation. He learned a lot more about what his children had been up to in the last two years than he had in all of their visits. They all felt more relaxed here than in the hospital room and Hector was starting to think this move was a good idea.

After dinner, the boys all ran to play in the living room and the adults stayed at the table, talking about what was going to be going on now that Hector was home.

"Do you have anyone medical coming in to care for him, Mom?" Gianna had both of her legs pulled up and crossed on the dining room chair, sipping on a cup of tea.

"Mrs. Gunnerson, two houses down, remember her? She offered to come over a couple times a week to check on him. She's a retired nurse and said she'd be happy to do it."

Frannie finished clearing the table and walked into the kitchen, knowing that she was going to receive some grief from her daughter.

"Mom, you need someone with medical training from *this* decade. Someone that has experience with comas and feeding tubes. What kind of nurse was she?"

Frannie thought for a minute, not actually sure of the answer. She walked back into the dining room with a plate of cookies. "I eh, I don't know. I didn't ask, I just appreciated the offer."

Angelo, Dominic, and Sage all looked at Gianna, waiting for her response but to their disappointment, never got it. Gianna just shook her head, grabbing a cookie and looked into the living room at the kids playing.

It was Angelo that jumped in next, "We can do some research, find someone that can come to the house and check on dad every day. Someone that can take some of the stress off of you."

Dominic nodded, adding in, "It'll help, Mom, I promise. You and I, we can watch him but if something went wrong, we wouldn't know what to do. If he started losing his hair or growing huge moles all over his body, the only thing we have is Google and that's not good enough for dad. I agree we need to get a real, current nurse."

"Yes, Fran, a real nurse can do everything you shouldn't be doing. It's one thing to have a person being paid to take care of you; it's another for your wife to have to. Please, Frannie, listen to them. They're right this time. You need help. You shouldn't be doing this anyway."

Frannie sat down, listening to her adult children talk about what they would like in a nurse and what their expectations were on care. She was grateful that her kids wanted to help and she knew they were right. She needed help but she had a hard time asking for it. Frannie looked over at Hector, hoping and praying for this two-year nightmare to be over. This new step seemed like one in the right direction, one that would pave the way for Hector's recovery.

It wasn't until the house cleared and everyone but Frannie had gone to bed that Hector started feeling the guilt spread through his body. The events of the day had left Hector on cloud nine but slowly reality came crashing down. He knew Frannie never stayed up late but he heard her one room away, listening to low music and flipping the pages of a book on the sofa that they had picked out together many years ago. Hector's idea of complete comfort was a brown leather La-Z-Boy recliner his father had that he needed special permission to sit in. He had always wanted one of his own but in red and after Dominic had been old enough to not destroy the furniture; Frannie surprised Hector by letting him pick one out. The only catch was that she wanted a whole new living room set to match. Hector took the deal and within a few weeks, they had custom furniture and a new La-Z-Boy recliner that he spent most of the next few years in.

He wasn't sure why she was still awake but the thought that it had anything to do with him made him sad. He knew this was going to be hard, he knew that Frannie and Dominic would struggle with the care and he wished he could make the decision to go back to the facility. This way, he would only be a thought when they came to visit him, instead of a constant reminder of the money sucking, time-consuming leech he was on their lives. Feeling the guilt of his presence, Hector tried anything to get himself to wake up, to move, to do anything. He was breathing on his own so why couldn't he move anything else?

Hector focused on one part of his body, his eyes. He thought about looking around at the room, he thought about opening his eyelids to see his beautiful wife looking down at him. He focused all his energy on getting his eyelids to lift and his eyes to look up. He thought about being able to see his family again, to see what his grandsons looked like now and to see the house he was in. He thought about how opening his eyes would be one step closer to being the man he used to be, the man his family needed. While focusing his attention and energy on his eyes, Hector felt another part of his body beg for attention. He felt so close to opening his eyes that he didn't want to give up just yet, he pushed just a little bit harder and to his surprise, his eyelids fluttered open, just for a brief second, barely long enough to see Frannie jumping off of the sofa, a look of panic on her face, running over to him.

"Frannie! You saw them, right?! You saw my eyes open, please tell me you saw my eyes open."

Hector had been so focused on opening his eyes that he didn't hear the alarms on his heart monitor going off.

Frannie got to Hector's side, looking over at the monitor as Dominic came running down the stairs. They both stood in the dining room, looking between Hector and the equipment for a moment before Dominic went to his dad's side. He lifted his hand and pushed the pulse oximeter more securely onto his finger just as Hector's body started to calm down. The alarm went off for a few more seconds before returning to its normal rhythm. Dominic set his dad's hand down gently and walked over to his Mom, his body shaking.

"Do you think something actually happened or it wasn't on his finger right…?"

"I don't know. Everything seems okay now; maybe it slipped off his finger just enough to not record anything?"

Frannie was hoping she was right. It was only the first night and they already had alarms going off. She could only think about how this was a bad sign. "Do you think we made a mistake? You think he should have stayed at Hope Covenant?" Frannie was worried that this was just the beginning of Hector's downfall.

"I don't know, Mom. I want to say I think he's getting better. I mean, he is breathing on his own and that's a big deal. There's no way he could have stayed there. With all the mistakes? No way. Do you think he moved his finger and it knocked it a little?" Dominic was reaching but Frannie appreciated his optimism.

"Maybe. I didn't see anything though. I ran in as soon as the alarms started going off. Maybe it was just a malfunction or like you said, the monitor wasn't on his finger enough. I'll sleep on the sofa tonight so I can be right here just in case it goes off again. I'll call for you if I need your help, okay?" Frannie smiled over at Dominic, grabbing his hand and squeezing it.

"Frannie, you don't have to sleep on the couch, I promise to not stress myself out. Frannie…you don't have to do any of this."

Hector mentally kicked himself for pushing too hard. He had caused more unnecessary stress for his wife, something he really didn't want to do.

"Thank you for being here, Dom. I really…really appreciate it. I do need help, so…thank you." Against her better judgment, Frannie let a little bit of doubt come out. "I don't know if I can do this, Dom. I don't think I thought this through. I was just so angry with Hope Covenant, I made a decision…and I don't know if it was the right one. I don't know if he'll ever get better…" Frannie felt tears threatening to escape but quickly pushed them away, not wanting to show her regret in front of her son.

"I am getting better, I promise. Please stay with me, please believe in me. I just opened my eyes! I saw you, Frannie, I saw you coming towards me. You look as beautiful

as the day I met you. It may have cost me a little heart thing...whatever it was, but I got to see your face, Frannie."

He could imagine the tears in her eyes just from hearing the tremble in her voice. It reminded him of when they first started dating. He'd snuck over to her house and gently tapped on the window, waving her outside with a smile after she peeked through the curtain. Frannie had giggled and shook her head but came outside in the rain anyway. The raindrops fell onto her cheeks and ran down them as Hector flipped the hood of his jacket up, enveloping them in their own world. In the early morning hours, while no one else was awake, Frannie and Hector stood in the driveway, exchanging long passionate kisses.

"I would do it all over again just to see you looking at me. I wish you would have seen it, I need you to know I'm here."

Hector knew that trying to open his eyes right now to prove that he was there was out of the question. His body couldn't take it, and Hector needed to be more careful.

Dominic reached over and kissed his mom's cheek. "We've got this, Mom. I'm here to help you. Derrick will be here soon. We'll be here to help you through everything. I know Gianna and Angelo will be too. Just let us know when you need the help." Frannie nodded while Dominic hugged her. He stole one last look at his dad before he headed towards the stairs, disappearing up to the second floor.

Frannie watched him until she couldn't see him anymore then sat on the end of Hector's bed, looking at him. "Darling, I want to do well. I want to be good for you. Please get better, please. I cannot lose you. I know this isn't how we imagined our lives or our home. I know we wanted to watch the grandkids grow up; we wanted to travel to places we've never been. We had a whole life still ahead of us. We can still do it; you just need to wake up. Hector, please…" Frannie let her tears flow while looking down at her lap. Shuddering with every breath she wiped at her eyes.

Hearing his wife cry this way and not being able to hold her could have killed Hector. He hated hearing her so sad and to know it was because of him was overwhelming. He knew he had to get better for her or leave this world entirely.

"Hector, I need you. I need you to be here with me, I cannot do this all by…" Frannie lost her train of thought as she heard what song was on the radio. She smiled even though more tears started to fall.

"You hear it, baby? It's our song. This has to be a sign, right?" Frannie started singing along to "Faithfully," memories of their first dance on their wedding night swirling in her head. Her white, beaded dress swaying to the music, pushed up against Hector's classic black tuxedo. She remembered the feel of the satin lapel against her cheek as they danced and the smell of white carnation with blue tipped petals filled her nose. "I remember you singing this into my ear when we were dancing. I didn't care that everyone was watching us. All I cared about was that I was finally marrying you. After all those years, playing together as kids, I finally was marrying you, Hector. You're all I ever wanted. You were…" She stopped herself, "…are everything I need." She slid forward on the bed, lying down next to him, her head on his shoulder, softly singing the words to her husband.

"Oh girl, you stand by me. I'm forever yours, faithfully. I will always be yours, Frannie, always."

Hector would have given anything to be able to dance to their song with his wife at that moment, but the most he could do was feel the tear slide down from his eye. Even this being a cruel joke that life was playing on him because the tear was on the side of his face opposite from where Frannie was so she didn't see it.

Drying her face, she did one more check of Hector's monitors before kissing his cheek and whispering her goodnight. She gathered up some blankets and made a bed for herself on the sofa, wanting to be closer to her husband.

"Goodnight, Sweetheart. I love you with everything I have left."

Hector knew Frannie meant well but knowing she wasn't up in their bed and hearing her desperate plea made Hector feel even worse for causing this scare. He wanted to move and he wanted to keep trying, but not when he knew what could happen. He had to work at this slowly, to make sure his heart could handle it. For the first time in a long time, Hector felt as if he had a chance at a physical recovery.

Snuggled into the couch, Frannie listened to the wind outside, the Cuckoo clock in the hallway and the new beeping coming from the dining room. The eggshell walls and the natural hardwood floors only amplified the sounds in the house. They echoed off every surface and mocked the empty feeling she already had. She couldn't sleep, but that was nothing new to her. The weight of her decision to bring Hector home sat on her chest and the thought of the trial happening in a few days was enough to make Frannie want to crawl out of her skin. She was worried about the alarm that had gone off. What if it wasn't the monitor on his finger? What if something actually had gone wrong and she wasn't doing anything about it? She wouldn't be able to live with herself if something happened to Hector because of her.

Frannie could hear Hector's breathing; his natural breathing and she noticed that as she started to drift off to sleep that both her and Hector's breath had matched in rhythm and rate. Thinking about each other and wishing; they would do anything to be together again.

Chapter 8

Frannie and Angelo sat in silence, waiting for their lawyer to come into the small conference room off to the side of the courtroom. She hadn't slept or eaten in days, the knots in her stomach making it hard to focus on anything other than the trial. She wasn't sure what to expect, she didn't know what would happen today, but she knew she had to face the man that put her husband into a coma and she wasn't ready for that. Angelo's leg bounced with impatience and his hands fidgeted with the sleeves of his jacket. Just as Angelo was about to say something, the heavy door swung open and Mr. Milano walked in with his briefcase.

"Hi folks, how are you?"

Frannie nodded with a polite but nervous smile and Angelo stood to shake his hand, "We're fine. How are you? Are we all set for today? We're actually doing this?"

"Yes, we have everything we need, the company has their lawyer here and as far as I know, all the witnesses are here." Angelo sat back down, nodding. Mr. Milano pulled a chair in front of the two of them, "I want to prepare you for what you're going to hear. They will go over the entire accident multiple times, what happened before and what happened after. They will ask a lot of questions of the witnesses and you'll have to hear about it from multiple views. This will be hard, very hard and you'll want to leave," He looked at Frannie as he said this, "but I need you to stay and be strong. I need you to be a united front, all of you." Now he looked over at Angelo for this next part, "There will be no interruptions, no yelling, no aggressive signs of emotion. Okay?"

Both Frannie and Angelo nodded, wanting nothing more than for this to be over and to get justice for Hector. Frannie still didn't know if the man who did this did it on purpose or if it was an accident, she would like to think it was just a bad accident, but she knew she had to prepare for the worst.

"Frannie? Are you ready?"

Frannie snapped out of her thoughts, realizing that both her son and lawyer were waiting at the door for her.

"Yes, sorry. I'm ready." She took a deep breath and stood, walking through the door and into the courtroom. She felt as if she were floating; like she wasn't actually there. She looked around the dark wooden room and saw her other children in the audience along with Derrick and Sage. Frannie felt small in the room that had large, over constructed pieces of furniture on different levels. She looked up at the judge, a slender man with a very angular face and glasses that seemed to be too small. His hair was barely more than a wisp and was white as the snow. She could tell that in his younger years his eyes would have caught the attention of any girl but in his age, she saw the years of hard decisions and heartache.

She was happy that she had such a supportive family but she wished she didn't have to be in this situation at all. She followed Angelo into a seat right behind her lawyer and his partner. Angelo's leg resumed its bouncing and Frannie turned her head towards the defendant's side. She spotted Paul talking to the lawyer and noticed he looked pale. Normally Paul was a tall, tanned man with thinning blond hair. He had a stocky frame but was not at all unhealthy and his personality was the exact opposite of his appearance. If she actually knew Paul like she thought she did, she knew that a courtroom was not a place he wanted to be. She could tell he was nervous and she almost felt bad until she remembered how he hadn't been cooperating with the investigation so she turned away, not wanting him to see her staring.

"Mom, do you know which one did it?" Gianna was leaning forward past her mom, scrutinizing every man she saw, not knowing who worked with Hector and who didn't.

"No, I don't. I don't know his name. I actually don't even know it's a he really, I guess I'm just assuming." Frannie started looking at everyone, wondering if the person that caused the accident was there yet. She wanted to prepare herself so when the person took the stand, she wasn't caught off guard but there was no way to know. Mr. Milano turned around, looked around at the family and gave them all a smile, everyone nodded back at him as they stood for the judge.

Through most of the trial, Frannie sat quietly, desperately trying to understand what was going on. She watched the lawyers give their opening statements to the jury, the corporate side talking about workplace accidents, as unfortunate as they are, they still happen and that's all that happened here. Her lawyer took a different approach. He talked about Hector, about his life and his family. He talked about how even though workplace accidents do happen, there should still be some accountability from the company. Mr. Milano talked about how Hector was still in a coma after two years. How his life had changed because of something that happened in his workplace and Frannie watched as all the jurors followed him with their eyes, waiting for what was coming next.

Frannie watched them address the judge and watched as they called their witnesses. The first few witnesses were employees that were there at the time of the accident, all of them telling their side of the story, what they heard, what they saw. They told the court about the amount of blood around Hector and the sound of the parts hitting bone. Her lawyer had been right, Frannie wanted to run away. She wasn't sure if it was from the turning of her stomach, her inability to breathe or the tunnel vision that had started. She didn't want to hear the testimony; she didn't want to hear the story over and over again. Frannie could only imagine the horror it would have been to watch these huge racks tilting and large, heavy parts starting to fall onto someone you worked with. Her heart hurt for all these people that had to watch this happen but it broke for Hector. She knew the horror of the accident from her side, getting the phone call that something had happened to her husband, but she couldn't fathom what it was like to be buried by steel without much of a warning.

Being in the courtroom brought Frannie back to the day of the accident and the phone call she'd received when the accident happened. She was at school and having a great day. She felt positive and optimistic as she worked with a small boy who had been under her care for a couple years now when the assistant principal, Mr. Haltom, came into the classroom. Frannie didn't look up; she was focused on helping the child color in the lines of his workbook when she felt a hand on her shoulder.

"Mrs. Plata, there's an urgent phone call for you in the office. It's from your husband's job." Frannie told the child she would be back in a couple minutes and walked with Mr. Haltom back to the office in silence. Frannie couldn't read the situation but the hairs on her arms stood up, panic slowly coursing through her body with every step. Hector had never called her at school like this, so she knew something happened. Mr. Haltom led her into his office and shut the door behind her, giving her some privacy. She picked up the phone expecting her husband on the other end.

"Frannie? It's Paul. Frannie, Hector's been in an accident. He's on his way to St. Joe's right now. You're going to want to meet him there. I'm so sorry Frannie but you need to get there right now."

Frannie started to shake, her mind flying to the worst case scenario. "Paul, what happened? Is he okay?"

"No. He's not. I'm so sorry. I don't know what else to say. Please go to the hospital, I'll meet you there."

Frannie hung up the phone, everything in the room feeling a thousand miles away. She tried to stand up but her legs felt like Jell-O and she had to steady herself. She felt like she was going to stop breathing but she had to go to the hospital. She ran to the door, quickly explained to Mr. Haltom what was going on then left. Frannie wasn't sure how she got to the hospital, she doesn't remember driving there but she knew she had. She called Angelo on the way, telling him that his father had been in an accident and to let the other kids know where he was going to be. Frannie pulled into a spot and took off running towards the ER entrance. She spotted Paul right inside the doors and ran to him.

"Frannie, the doctors are with him, he's being prepped for surgery."

Frannie's knees wanted to give out and Paul helped her to a chair. "What happened, Paul? What's going on?"

"I don't know exactly, but I know some racks were knocked over and the parts on those racks fell onto him. Frannie, I don't want to scare you, but I'm scared, he didn't look good." Paul put his head in his hands, shaking his head. "I'm so sorry, Fran, I don't know anything else. I just heard the racks falling and ran out. There were guys moving the parts and we called 9-1-1. It all happened so fast."

She wanted to keep listening to him but it felt as if her ears stopped working. Her body trying to shut down to save her from the shock and pain of what was going on. She interrupted him, "Can we see him? You said he's going into surgery? What surgery?" She couldn't believe what was going on but her thoughts were quickly brought back to the courtroom when she felt Gianna grab her arm.

The company lawyer, Ms. Wimbley, a tall, slim woman with all the right curves and an attitude that screamed confidence wore a navy-colored suit with a pencil skirt that accentuated her assets. Frannie never liked judging a book by its cover but she could instantly tell that this woman knew how men responded to her and had no trouble using it to her advantage. She had called a man to the stand, dressed in a suit that looked too old and too big to actually be his. Frannie had missed the man being sworn in but she was very aware of the answer he was giving the lawyer.

"Yes Ma'am, I was driving the Hilo that hit the racks." He seemed nervous and had a hard time keeping eye contact with anyone. Frannie's breath caught in her throat and she grabbed back at her daughter.

"That's him? He's the one that was driving? What was his name?" Frannie whispered to Gianna who had been paying attention the whole time.

Gianna nodded, her eyes not coming off of that man at the stand. "Frank McMullen."

The lawyer walked in front of the man and towards the jury. "Mr. McMullen, can you please explain to the jury what a Hilo is?"

Frank nodded and angled himself more towards the jury box, "A Hilo is a forklift, it's eh...it's just a different name that we call them. It's a vehicle that we use in the plant to move heavy parts or really anything that's heavy. We use it a lot." He looked at the lawyer, then down at his hands.

"Mr. McMullen, you regularly drive these forklifts, correct?"

Frank nodded, looking up at the lawyer and quickly adding in, "Yes Ma'am. I do almost every day."

"Can you tell the court what happened the day of Hector Plata's accident?"

Frank looked to be visibly shaking and Frannie started to feel bad for being mad at someone without knowing the whole story. This man looked awful, like he had been beating himself up for this since it happened and Frannie decided that she already believed it was an accident.

"Yes. I eh…I came into work like normal, like every day and I worked on a few other things that morning but someone needed me to get a part for them so I got on the forklift." Frank's voice was shaky and quiet leaving Frannie with an overwhelming desire to hug him. She didn't know why after two years of hatred she was suddenly softening. "The forklift started up like normal, everything seemed fine…but when I tried to stop…it didn't. I pressed on the brake but nothing happened. I tried to yell to everyone to watch out, but sometimes we wear headphones." Frank looked down at his hands again and Frannie wanted to cry. This whole time it has been an accident and not only was Hector's life changed, but she knew that Frank's had too.

"Mr. McMullen, are the forklifts regularly inspected?" Ms. Wimbley looked from the jury back to her witness then over her shoulder to Mr. Milano.

"Yes. They should be. They get inspected once a month."

"And Mr. McMullen, when was the last time this particular forklift had been inspected at the time of the accident?"

"A little over a month before. It was overdue for an inspection, but I didn't know this at the time. I just grabbed one that was close to me." Frank shook his head like he was preparing to get into trouble.

"So it wasn't part of your routine to check the inspections. Mr. McMullen, can you tell the court who was supposed to be keeping up with the inspections on these forklifts, please?"

Frank was quiet for a minute and Frannie hung onto the silence before he said, "Hector Plata was the inspector." At that moment, the air left the courtroom as most of the crowd gasped. Frannie couldn't believe that right now, Hector looked like he was responsible for his own accident.

"So you're saying that if Mr. Plata had done his job correctly, this situation could have been avoided and both your lives could have gone on as normal?"

"Objection! Your Honor, she's leading the witness." Mr. Milano stood up as he talked.

Frannie looked between the witness and the lawyer then over at Angelo who appeared to be fighting his own body to stay in his seat.

"Sustained. Counsel, move on, please."

Ms. Wimbley nodded and moved on with her questioning but Frannie had a hard time focusing on anything other than the thought of Hector. She thought about how he was home with a new nurse that he didn't know, and she wondered if he was even aware of the change in company. All she wanted to do was go home and hug him. She wanted to tell him she was sorry he had to go through any of this. The recounting of his accident gave her a clearer picture of what happened and it was devastating. After almost an hour more of questioning from the company's side, it was finally time for Mr. Milano to question Frank.

"Hi Mr. McMullen, can you please tell the court what your workplace relationship to Mr. Plata was?"

"It eh…I barely knew him. I knew he had been there a long time but I didn't really know him good. We didn't really run in the same circle." Frank looked over at his lawyer, searching for some support but not getting any.

"So there would be no reason for you to want to harm Mr. Plata?"

"What? No! I barely knew him. I don't want to hurt anyone..." Frank's eyes went wide, looking from Mr. Milano to the jury and back to his lawyer.

Frannie didn't know where her lawyer was going but she knew it was making Frank nervous. She looked over towards the other lawyers and noticed they were furiously writing notes while watching the interaction between Frank and Mr. Milano.

"So is it true that just a few weeks before the accident, you were written up for an outburst directed at Mr. Plata?" Frank looked confused for a moment then realization spread across his face.

"No...I never...wait..." Frannie watched as Frank deflated, remembering the incident and she wondered if this was the same guy that accused Hector of stealing his lunch a few weeks before the accident. It had been a story that they laughed over but Frannie didn't realize it had been serious enough for Frank to be written up.

"So it is true? You and Mr. Plata had an altercation at work? Can you tell us about it?" Mr. Milano walked back towards the desk then turned around, waiting for Frank's answer.

"Yes sir, but it was so stupid and dumb. I eh…we were in the lunchroom and my lunch was gone. I had been in a lot of pain with my back, I don't know what I did to it, but it hurt so I was really pissy…er…mad, but someone had touched my lunch and I just lost it. Hec…Mr. Plata just happened to be by the fridge and I thought it was him. He eh, he kept telling me that he didn't touch it and I…I pushed him into the fridge." Frannie shook her head, this wasn't the story that Hector told her. All Hector said was that the guy yelled at him but his lunch had been in the fridge the whole time. He laughed when he told the story; he never told her it had gotten physical.

"Did Mr. Plata retaliate?"

"No, he just walked away and told me to check the fridge again…my lunch was just pushed to the back…" Frank looked down at his hands, shame emanating from his face.

"So you did know Mr. Plata and he made you look like a fool in front of your co-workers. Were you mad at him after that?"

"Well...yeah but not mad enough to do anything...I didn't push the racks over on purpose! It was an accident, I told you already. The brakes went out, I pushed the brake over and over but it just wouldn't stop." Frank was practically yelling at this point and the Judge told him to calm down.

"Is it also true that you failed a drug test after the incident?"

"Objection, Your Honor. The test was dismissed and ruled inadmissible due to a break in the chain of custody."

"Sustained"

"I have no more questions, Your Honor." Mr. Milano turned back towards the Plata family, giving them a nod before he sat back down.

After Frank left the stand, the Judge called for a lunch recess. Frannie and her family stayed seated until the courtroom emptied. Frannie knew she had to be the strong one for her children but she was having a hard time coming up with any words for what they all just sat through. She wasn't sure if anything she said would take the forlorn look off their faces so she did all she could do, she stood up and led the way out of the courtroom.

In the hallway, Angelo was the first one to say anything, "So, is anyone hungry? We should eat something." Everyone nodded a bit but had no real intention of eating.

***

They found a small diner around the corner from the courthouse, ordered their meals and watched as they grew cold. Dominic sat next to Frannie, pushing around a bit of rice on his plate, "Mom, do you think he's telling the truth? Do you think it was really an accident?"

Frannie thought for a moment, wanting it to be true but knowing that not everything is what it seems. "I don't know. I want to believe him. He looks so sad. I can't really imagine what he's been going through the last two years…"

"What he's been going through? Mom, listen to yourself. What about what we've been going through? Our dad is the one that's been gone for the last two years, Frank's still alive!" Angelo tried to keep his voice down as to not cause a scene but he had been fighting this back all day.

"Your dad is alive, Angelo. He is not dead so stop talking like he is." Frannie felt frozen, as if time had stopped. She wanted to get up from the table and leave the diner, to be by herself, or better yet, to be with Hector. She believed that he was getting better and she didn't want to hear her children talk like he wasn't even alive but despite what she wanted, she knew what her kids needed. "I know it would be easier to give up, believe me, I've wanted to give up too but we are so close to the end of this and your dad is getting better. He's breathing on his own now, that is a huge step. We just need to keep doing what we're doing. We need to be there for your dad. Okay?"

All three of her children were looking down at their plates and it reminded her of when they were younger and one of them broke a glass on the end table. None of them had fessed up to doing it and Hector was talking to them at the dinner table, their heads bowed in the same way as they were now. Gianna looked up at her mom with tears in her eyes, nodding her head.

"Mom, we're trying. We've all been trying. We're here for you and dad now, but we're allowed to be upset. This is hard. Hearing what happened to dad, it's hard to listen to." Angelo put his arm around his sister and she leaned her head onto his shoulder. Frannie knew that she was right, that her children were allowed to be upset, that she was allowed to be upset.

"Let's head back to the courthouse; they should start up again soon." Dominic slid out of the booth, looking back at the table, almost none of the food eaten.

***

Ms. Wimbley approached the bench, "We'd like to call to the stand Paul Lavoy." Paul stood up and adjusted the jacket of the only suit Frannie knew he owned as he made his way to the stand, being the defendant's next witness. He was sworn in and Frannie could see the fear and stress on his face. Even after everything he'd done, or not done in Frannie's mind, she still felt a pang of guilt in her chest, wishing that Paul would have just been on their side throughout the whole situation. She thought about how great he was in the hospital the day of the accident, how he had been next to her the whole time. She had struggled with the thought of Paul being against Hector, but now she would know for sure what had happened.

"Mr. Lavoy, you're Mr. Plata's supervisor, correct?"

Paul nodded, "You're correct, Ma'am."

"You are one of his friends, is that correct also?"

"Yes, that is also correct." Paul sat with his hands folded in his lap, his face pale and his eyes glued to Ms. Wimbley.

As the questioning continued for another 30 minutes Frannie watched as Paul took longer and longer breaks before answering them. She watched the movement in his eyes, constantly looking down or being closed. She knew something was wrong, she could see him starting to sweat.

"Mr. Lavoy, can you please tell the court the kind of worker Frank McMullen is?" After this was asked, Frannie and Paul's eyes met, she saw the tears starting to pool on his bottom lids and gave him a questioning look. He stared at her for a few seconds before looking over at Frank, then to the lawyer.

"I can't do this."

"We're almost done, Mr. Lavoy..."

"No..." Paul interrupted the lawyer. "This. Any of this. None of it is the truth. The brakes worked fine, Hector had just inspected them the week before and I signed off on the report. I know I signed that report. Hector was a fantastic employee and he never missed an inspection, you told me the report wasn't in the system, but I knew it had happened. Frank is not telling the truth and neither are you."

"Now Mr. Lavoy, I understand this is stressful but you swore to tell the truth, the whole truth and nothing but the truth." The lawyer walked back to her desk and Frannie noticed that when she did, she made eye contact with Frank, who looked as if he'd seen a ghost.

"I am telling the truth, this should have been told years ago." Paul turned to Mr. Milano, "The truth is that Frank was on something that wasn't his. I don't know what, but he told me last week, he was high. That test was right, it came back positive." The lawyer whipped around to look at Frank, her eyes wide before quickly turning back around towards Paul.

Frannie felt her face start to burn as the heat rose through her cheeks. She knew something was wrong, and she knew that Paul was keeping secrets, she just couldn't believe that he would have done this to her family.

"Mr. Lavoy right now is not the time to start telling stories…" Ms. Wimbley now looked as if she was standing on needles, her face was pinched and her hands tight to her sides.

"I'm not telling stories…you lied."

"Objection, Your Honor. The jury shouldn't be hearing this. This contradicts all of our statements." Ms. Wimbley tried to keep her cool but she was slowly unraveling.

"Overruled. Let the witness speak"

"But Your Honor, this can't…" Before she could finish her sentence the Judge cut her off by leaning towards her, covering the microphone.

"Counsel, if you don't let him speak, I'll find you in contempt." The Judge turned towards Paul, "Mr. Lavoy, please tell me what you're talking about."

Before Paul started talking he looked over at Frannie again, an apologetic look across his face, "Your Honor, Frank came into my office last week, he…he told me that the test wasn't wrong. That he and Ms. Wimbley covered it up. I had no idea, I didn't know that there was anything to the accident besides bad brakes, even though I know Hector did the inspection. Stuff happens all the time, brakes go bad…but I didn't know any of this until last week, I promise. I thought some things were weird, like the missing report but no one is perfect, I guessed that Hector could have forgotten but it wasn't like him...I trusted Ms. Wimbley, I trusted that she was going to help us all." Paul was unraveling, all of the anxiety and stress from this secret-spilling out into the courtroom. Frannie watched as her children followed every word, their faces showing every emotion that went through their minds. She looked over at Ms. Wimbley who was stone-faced, sitting in her chair behind the desk. Her partner looking between her and Paul.

"Frank told me that he had taken one of his friend's pills for his back and when he came into work the next day...he was still intoxicated. Your Honor, I didn't know what to do. This has been eating me up inside." Paul was breaking down on the stand. Frannie saw tears streaming down his face and realized that she had tears on her own cheeks. "I never wanted to keep any secrets, especially from the Plata family. I just keep thinking that if I noticed he was intoxicated, all of this could have been avoided." Paul turned to Frannie, "Frannie, I'm so sorry...I should have told you, I should have kept him safe, I'm so sorry...I promise I didn't know..." Frannie shook her head at Paul, wanting to jump up and hug him. She hated that she doubted him.

"Okay, okay. This has been enough for the day. Jurors, it seems that your duty for this case has changed. Counsel, I need to see you in my chambers. The court is dismissed." Ms. Wimbley looked at her partners, her jaw clenched and her hands in fists. Mr. Milano looked back at the family, a look of disbelief on his face as he headed towards the office door.

Frannie sat in silence and shock, looking down the line of her children who were all looking to her for answers. She didn't know what to think or expect. Instead of the trial coming to an end, it seemed now to have just started. She opened her mouth to speak but nothing came out.

Chapter 9

The anniversary of Hector's accident came days after the trial. What she thought was going to be a hard day turned out to be like any other. As much as she tried, Frannie still couldn't wrap her head around anything that had actually happened in the courtroom. She went to work and had a relatively normal day. Amelia had made strides in her progress and her parents had credited Frannie with that. Frannie was incredibly happy to be so involved in someone else's life but she had to admit it was for selfish reasons. She was tired of focusing on her life; she was tired of always worrying about things and having those things go wrong anyway. She loved being able to focus on the happiness that was Amelia's progress. She loved the daily victories and she loved to see the smile of her face when Amelia was praised for her good behavior.

Frannie often felt guilty about it, but sometimes she would sit in her car in the parking lot just 15 minutes longer than normal before starting the car and heading home. When she came home the sight of Hector was a constant reminder of a mistake she was fighting within herself. She had mentioned her fears to Dominic once but after that, they were never talked about again. It wasn't that she didn't want to help, but as her children warned her, this was a lot more work than she thought and she was struggling to keep up. She took care of her husband with the help of her son but the guilt and anxiety that eventually started seeping into her body were getting to be too much.

Frannie didn't want a large family dinner and she didn't really want to talk about what today meant. Last year

Frannie had spent the anniversary by Hector's side but it was almost too painful. This anniversary wasn't something to be celebrated. Like everything else in her life, Frannie felt guilty for not spending the day with Hector. It was too painful and she didn't want to spend the day looking over at her husband, thinking about what had happened a few years ago. She didn't want to replay the phone call in her head anymore or how she watched him after his surgeries and she didn't want to think about how much time had passed since she had been able to hear his voice. Hector's voice was something Frannie never grew bored with. The smooth bass with a hint of Spanish accent drove her wild and throughout the years, Frannie would call his cell phone just to hear his voicemail.

She also had made a habit of saving voicemails on her phone from everyone she loved. She had ones from all her children, her parents and from Hector. His voicemail was one that always made her laugh. It started off with him asking her to call him back because he forgot the list for the grocery store but it quickly turned into his rendition of Happy Birthday. The list he needed was simple, balloons and her cake. Hector always had a way of turning routine things into grand gestures and Frannie missed that about him.

When Frannie walked in the door of her house she heard Dominic and Derrick, who had arrived a few days before, talking in the living room. This was normal for her now but what stood out was a third man's voice. She couldn't quite make out what any of them were saying but she hesitated as she walked around the corner to see that Paul Lavoy was sitting on her sofa. Her heart sank as she saw the sad expression on his face when he looked up at her. She knew that he hadn't been involved in the cover-up or the lying but she was still angry with him for keeping that secret from her. She stood in the entryway to the living room for a moment before Derrick noticed she was there, following Paul's look.

"Oh hi, Ma. Paul came over to see Dad. He wanted to talk to you too." She could tell that Derrick was a little hesitant. He knew the relationship that Paul had with the family and was there at the trial when all the secrets came out.

Frannie nodded and moved into the kitchen, hanging her keys and purse up on the hooks right inside the door. Paul walked in a moment later, his hands tangled together in front of him, a sign that he felt uncomfortable. She turned toward him without saying a word.

"Frannie, we need to talk. Please?"

She remained quiet but led him into the dining room to a chair. Dominic and Derrick took this as their cue to give them some privacy and made their way out of the house. Paul glanced over at Hector as he walked into the room then back at Frannie.

"Do you think he can hear us?"

"Of course I can hear you, go ahead, talk to her and tell her what you told me. She told me everything that happened at the trial. I'm glad you finally said something."

Hector had been mad but relieved that Paul told the truth. He had also been working on opening his eyes, a little bit further along each time he tried. He had to be very cautious about his heart rate when he did this though, he could feel the strain it was putting on it and he didn't want the alarms to go off and scare his family again. At this point, he could move his eyeballs up and down but not open his eyelids without alarms. Each day, he worked a little harder on opening his eyes or moving his fingers, one step closer to once again being able to tell Frannie that he loved her.

"Yes, I do. At every scan, he has brain activity and to me, that means he can hear us. No one has told me otherwise so that's what I choose to believe." Frannie sat down at the table, across from Paul and closest to Hector. "What do you want to talk about, Paul?" She looked across the table at him, seeing the desperation in his face.

"Frannie, you know I wanted to tell you about all that stuff, I just didn't know what to do. The company's lawyer was involved and I didn't know who to talk to about it..."

"Me, Paul. You talk to me. You tell me. You knew what happened to Hector, the truth about what happened, and you kept it quiet for a week?! Paul, you're supposed to be his friend, and that means being on our side, not against us. How do I even know that you only knew for a week?"

Paul looked down at his hands and took a deep breath. "I know, Fran. I'm sorry. I wanted to tell you that day in his room. I went there to talk to him, thinking that it might help me figure out what to do; I just didn't know how to say it. I couldn't find the right words for any of it. I just...this is so hard and I know it's hard for you too, I just didn't know what to do."

Frannie understood the position Paul was in but that didn't mean that she wasn't still mad at him. He had been Hector's friend for so long that she expected better from him, she expected him to help their family, not harm them.

"I know Paul. You just...you're his best friend. You should have told me, you should have let me know what was going on...he...no we, deserve that." Frannie was keeping it together, surprisingly. She felt like she was on the edge of a breakdown but she didn't want Paul to see that. "You could have warned me at least. You could have done something..."

"I did, Frannie. I told them the truth, I told them what I knew. No...it wasn't right away but I needed to process what I knew. I needed to make sure it all checked out. I had to give it time. I didn't want to upset you if it ended up being nothing. I know I hurt you and your family and I will never fully be able to apologize for that, but I'm so sorry that all of this had to happen." Paul was almost in tears now and Frannie had to look away to avoid her own. She went back and forth in her mind about what she wanted to do. She wanted to accept his apology and move on with her life but she was still so hurt by Paul. The last two years she had rarely seen or talked to him. After Hector's accident, Paul had all but disappeared from the Plata's lives and that also fueled her hurt.

She looked over at Hector and instantly remembered the time the whole family had gone with Paul up to the Silver Lake Sand Dunes in Northern Michigan. She remembered the sun and the lakes, the kids playing in the sand and the adults laughing over a cooler.

"Paul, do you remember when we went to the dunes?" Paul looked confused but nodded his head. "Do you remember that second night, around the fire after all the kids went to bed? We were talking about the future, about what we wanted for our kids, what we wanted for our own lives. The one thing Hector said he wanted was a life full of love and kindness. He said he wanted his family to never struggle, to never feel like they weren't loved and cared for. He wanted to put money away for his kids and grandkids. He had a whole plan that now can't happen." Frannie eased into a sad smile, "I tried to give him the best life he could have, before the accident. I tried to make sure we were always happy and I like to think that I did a good job at that..." She trailed off while her thoughts caught up with her and Paul shifted in his seat, watching Frannie talk.

"Hector was so happy and everyone loved him. He was always the center of attention and made everyone laugh and now...he just lies in a bed, pushed off to the side of the room while life keeps going without him." A hitch in her voice gave away her sadness and she turned towards Paul, tears starting to run down her cheeks. "Do you think that he is living his best life? Do you think..." She looked down at her hands, not really wanting to ask the next question.

"Frannie, you have done everything you can for Hector. You have made his life comfortable and the way you talk to him, I know he would appreciate and love that. You are the most amazing woman for everything you have done for your family. I know it's hard but what you've done so far has made a life for someone that had theirs stolen."

"You should listen to him, Fran. I would have never made it this far without you. I would have never started to get better if it weren't for your constant love and support."

Frannie looked over at Hector, dreaming of a day when he would be sitting next to her at the table, instead of lying still, looking like he's asleep in the middle of the day. "Thank you, Paul, it hasn't been easy and I have to admit, caring for him at home is…a lot harder than I thought it would be. Derrick and Dom have been so helpful but it's not fair that they are spending their days caring for him instead of out in the world, chasing their dreams. There was so much that went into this that I never even thought of. I took the facility and the nurses for granted and I should have never done that. Paul, I think I made a mistake…I shouldn't have brought him home with me…"

Paul cut Frannie off, not wanting her to say more, "It wasn't a mistake, maybe a lesson learned but definitely not a mistake. If you're rethinking the situation, you can always call Hope Covenant to see if they would have a place for him again or another facility, I know they don't have the best track record. No one will look down at you, Frannie. You have gone above and beyond to help Hector. No one will think any less of you." This was all Frannie needed to hear. She had been struggling with the thought that she would be giving up on Hector. She didn't want Hector to feel as if he was burdening her but she also didn't want people to think that she didn't care. She needed help and now she knew she could ask for it. Having Hector go back to a facility wasn't her giving up; it was Frannie helping herself before she could help anyone else. If she was at the end of her rope, there would be no rope to give anyone else.

"You're right. I need to call someone, to see if I can get him a room. There has to be more out there than Hope Covenant. I'll start researching to see where he could go; I just don't want to feel like I'm giving up. I'm not giving up on him, Paul, I promise."

"Oh Fran, I know you're not. You've done everything you could; you've actually done more than you should have. If I knew Hector at all, he wouldn't want you to struggle like this anymore. He wouldn't have wanted to you struggle at all." Paul stood up and walked over to Frannie, pulling her up into a hug. At first, Frannie held back, but after a moment she leaned into the hug and felt, even for a brief second that everything was going to work out.

"Please stick around. Don't disappear on me again. We need you in our lives. Hector needs you around. Come over for dinner sometime, you're always welcome here."

"I will, Fran. I'm sorry I was gone so long. I just couldn't forgive myself. I blamed myself for a long time. If I had not sent Hector to grab that part or if I had noticed that Frank wasn't right maybe none of this would have happened and Hector would still be around, still be the life of the party and the center of attention. I feel like I could have prevented this and it kills me that I didn't." Paul looked away from Frannie, wiping the tears in his eyes away before she could see them.

"If it makes a difference, I don't blame you at all. This was not and never has been your fault. This is Frank's fault, and I hope that this catches up with him." Frannie gritted her teeth for a moment but let her body relax, telling herself that she shouldn't worry about the situation until their next court date.

Frannie walked Paul to the door and after another hug, she watched him leave. She felt much better about their relationship and hoped that Paul would stick around this time. She never thought of it from his perspective. She never would have imagined that he had blamed himself for the accident but now that it was out there, she fully understood why. She had blamed him for a long time too, she'd had the same thoughts, but in her head, Paul hadn't even thought of Hector. It was a relief for her to realize that other people cared for Hector as much as her family did.

Frannie called Angelo and asked him to help her look over the proposed settlement that her lawyer had given to her the day before. The lawyer didn't say a word about it; he could only shake his head so she knew that this wasn't something she was going to like. With the trial drama and the insecurity about Paul behind her, she could now put all her focus on it. She wanted to read it over and decide what to do with Angelo's help.

A large pepperoni pizza and a couple of beers later, Frannie and Angelo sat at the dining room table, looking in disbelief over the settlement that was before them. Frannie now understood why Mr. Milano shook his head when she asked about it.

"Really? They don't want to claim any responsibility? How is this not their fault?!" Angelo sat shaking his head, rereading part of the settlement that a new lead lawyer for the company had given to them. "Sure, paying dad's medical bills is cool and this amount of money? Mom, we could do a lot with two hundred and fifty thousand, but really? Is it worth it for them to not claim responsibility? They would be getting off with no consequences. Frank would be just walking away...there's no way that can happen..." Angelo threw the pile of papers down on the table and took another drink of his beer.

"They can do better than this. I'm sure my medical bills are way more than 250 thousand at this point. Don't accept this Frannie, please don't agree."

Hector had been listening to his wife and son read different parts of the settlement out loud and that night he got to practice his eye rolling. He had hoped that at some point Frannie would be able to see his eyelids move but she had been so focused on the settlement that he didn't think she even looked over at him. He thought for a quick minute about pushing himself too far, just to get the alarms to go off for a moment but decided against it. He didn't want to add to the stress of the situation and definitely didn't want to scare Frannie again.

"Do you think we could get more? Is that greedy?" Frannie didn't know much about settlements but she knew that she wanted the company to take responsibility for the accident.

"We could definitely get more and no, that's not at all greedy. We have been through so much in the last two years.

They need to take responsibility, too. They can't just ignore that part. If they don't, then does that mean the accident was dad's fault?"

"I don't know. I don't know how all that works…" Frannie sighed and set the paperwork down. "We can deny this, though. We can tell them it isn't good enough for us. We have to have the upper hand here, right? There's no way, with all that stuff about covering up evidence and the drug test, there's no way that any of that has any legs to stand on. We should keep pushing forward."

Angelo looked at his mother, not expecting her to want to keep moving forward with the lawsuit. "I agree, Mom. We need to keep going. We need to do this for dad, he would have wanted us to do this and he would have wanted them to take responsibility."

Frannie nodded her head, picked up a sheet of paper and in an act fueled by maybe a little too much beer; she tore the page in half. It was more of a symbolic gesture, but it still made both her and Angelo feel good. They weren't going to accept this ridiculous deal; they wanted the company, the lawyer, and most of all Frank, to pay for what they have done to Hector. Frannie laughed after she threw the pages down, feeling very satisfied with herself.

"Oh Fran, dramatic much? Go get it, honey, tell them what you want. You guys have gone through so much in the last two years, you deserve everything they aren't willing to give you!"

Hector was proud of his wife and a little jealous that she was tipsy without him but pride took over. He couldn't wait to be there with her, to celebrate the victory of not only the lawsuit but of him waking up. He knew it was getting closer. He felt more in touch with his body every day. He just needed a little more time to connect with his muscles, to train them to do what he wanted them to do. As long as Frannie held out just a little longer, he would be with her for the rest of his life.

"Let's call Mr. Milano…tell him I said no deal!"

"Mom, it's almost 10 pm, how about we wait for the morning to call him? I'm sure he's not at the office right now." As Angelo talked, the front door opened, Dominic and Derrick walked through with takeout containers.

"Man, if we knew there was pizza here, we would have just come home before getting food…Thanks!" Dominic faked his anger as he walked by, flipping the lid of the box with half a pizza in it shut. "Well…if anyone is feeling Chinese, we got enough to share, unlike you two."

"Nah, I have to get home. I'm leaving this drunkard to you guys now." Angelo motioned towards his mother with a wink and a smile.

"I'm not drunk, I've had a couple of beers and I feel good about our situation. It's giving me a certain…not drunk feeling, but a good one." Frannie stood up and showed off her ability to walk in a straight line, proving to her boys that she was still of sound mind. "Anyway, I have to go to bed. I have lots of big calls to make tomorrow!" Frannie tipped her empty can at Angelo and walked up the stairs towards her bedroom.

"Eh...is Mom really drunk? What was she talking about? Big calls?" Dominic set out some of the takeout containers and grabbed for a few paper plates.

"The settlement that the other side sent to us, it's garbage. They don't want to take responsibility for dad's accident, they want to lowball us and move on like it never happened." Angelo picked up a piece of the ripped paper and showed it to Dominic. He held it up and looked at the torn edge. "Big gestures, Mom was full of dramatics tonight...it was the beer whether she wants to admit it or not."

"Well, at least she's confident, right? It's nice to see her not so wound up. She needs to relax every once in a while, she needs to let some of this go so we can help her." Dominic set the ripped paper back on the table with the rest of the scattered mess and went back into the kitchen where Derrick was picking through the containers with a set of chopsticks. "Angelo, you sure you don't want any?"

"Nah, I have to go home. Thanks, though. Make sure you keep an eye on her. I know she looks and feels good right now, but I have a feeling that in the morning it won't be the same story."

Dominic and Derrick nodded, knowing what Angelo was talking about. Frannie would sometimes get a burst of confidence to get something done but as quickly as it came, it went. Her children had come to expect this from her. It didn't make her a bad person and no one thought negatively about her, but they knew they had to be her confidence when it went away, which meant that Dominic and Derrick needed to remind her in the morning of all the reasons why she needed to make that call to deny this settlement.

Frannie sat up in her room on the side of the bed and thought about everything Hector has had to go through to get to where he was at. She felt guilty that the whole time she was in the dining room she basically ignored Hector like he wasn't even there. She didn't even say goodnight to him, which was something she always did. She stood up, deciding that it wasn't fair to go to bed without telling him goodnight when she very easily could. She snuck back downstairs, Dominic and Derrick in the living room, in front of the TV eating their take out. She made her way to the dining room quietly, not wanting to give herself away. Frannie walked up to Hector's bed and gasped, calling for Dominic. Both the men came running into the dining room and behind Frannie, let out gasps of their own.

"His eyes are moving, Mom...you can see them through his eyelids!"

"Frannie! You're here? I didn't hear you come in! You can see, I'm moving! I'm moving my eyes! I'm here baby, I'm here!"

"Hector...Please show me you're doing this. Please give me a sign that you're here and can hear me." Frannie looked desperately around Hector's body, watching to see if a finger moved or if a muscle twitched but to her disappointment, nothing else moved and his eyes stopped.

Hector desperately wanted to move more but he could feel his strength giving out.

He had been trying to move all night and now that his family was standing around him, he was too tired and too weak to prove to them that this was him, that he was moving his body parts. He screamed in his mind, he fought to continue to move but as he did he felt his heart starting to beat harder and he knew he had to stop unless he wanted them to take him back to the hospital and the hospital was where Hector knew his end could come.

"I don't see anything else, Mom but he was definitely moving his eyes...that couldn't have been a coincidence, right?" Dominic looked over at Derrick, who shrugged his shoulders.

"I don't think so Dom, I think he was doing that. He's getting better...I know he is. Go ahead and go back to your movie; I'll sit here a little longer. I want to see if anything else happens." Frannie pulled a chair over by Hector and shooed the two men away with her hand. She might have still been a little buzzed, but she knew what she'd seen and she was going to sit here in case it happened again. Frannie knew her husband was fighting and she was willing to fight for him and with him to get their lives back.

"Hector, I saw you. I know you're in there, baby, I know you're trying to get out. Please, please come out, Hector. Please come back to me." This was a plea that Frannie felt she has made a thousand times over but this time felt different. She had more hope for Hector's future and she felt like she could feel him waking up.

"I'm here Fran. I'm trying to be here with you. I just…something feels so wrong…something…something doesn't feel like I'm getting better. It feels like I'm getting worse…I feel so tired and so weak…"

Chapter 10

"You just need to let it go, Angelo! There's nothing we can do about it anymore. It's done! None of this will help anything." Gianna was yelling at her oldest brother over the kitchen island as he paced around the house.

"They cannot just get away with this! It's bullshit! Limited liability? What the hell is that? They can't even take responsibility for the accident! And Frank? Really? He gets a year of probation? *A year*? That's it? One year." Angelo looked as if he were about to explode. The family had just gotten back from the court date that was scheduled after the new information about Hector's case had come out. It had been less than a week but Frannie felt like an entire year had gone by with the amount of information that had been passed around and the speed of this case. Frank took a plea deal, giving up the company lawyer for covering up the drug test and lying in court and in return Frank was to participate in a 12-Step program and a year of probation instead of jail time.

Frannie watched as her eldest son stormed around the house, her daughter yelling at him and her middle son adding to the storm with his own anger. Paul sat beside Frannie at the kitchen table, feeling lost in the drama, not knowing if he should interject or sit in silence. He decided the best course of action was to let the family fight it out, being just a spectator.

"Gianna, look. This is absurd. Dad deserves more and that's why we're mad. The man who caused this accident, who came to work high, lied about it, covered up a drug test and kept it all a secret for almost two years is just walking away with probation and a class that he doesn't even really need! You heard the Judge, he said his record was clean. It may have been a one-time thing but that one-time thing caused our family all of this. Can't you see how that looks? How is that fair?" Dominic was sitting up on the counter and Frannie could tell he was holding back. "And the lawyer that helped with all this? Sure, she lost her job, was disbarred and her reputation is blown, but really…is that a fair consequence for this? No jail time, no nothing. She has to get a new job, that's it, while our dad is still lying in a bed. His entire life has been interrupted because of these people, and the best we get is the company saying that they maybe had a little responsibility in the accident? No, there's no way that's fair at all. There's no way that's how this is going to end!"

"Guys, I get it. I know how unfair it is, but really? Yelling and throwing a fit won't help any of it. It won't change any of it. You're wasting your energy." Gianna turned to her mom for support and backup.

"She's right. We've gone back and forth with them all week. I thought that 1.4 million was a ton of money but that's why we have Mr. Milano. He knows these cases better than us and you heard him. This was the best he could get for us. Your dad's medical bills are paid and will continue to be paid, which is a huge help. And now 5.5 million dollars..." Frannie took a deep breath, not really believing that amount herself, "...is way more than I even know what to do with. I know you want them to take more responsibility but this needs to be over. We can't do anything about Frank and that woman but hope that they see all the harm they've caused." Frannie couldn't say that she was happy about the limited liability part of the deal but she had to be done with it. Her lawyer had advised her that this deal was probably the best that was going to happen for her family. The important things like Hector's medical bills and their legal bills were covered; it had been the blame that Angelo and Dominic wanted the company to take that had been the hot topic of the week. Frannie didn't know how to convince her sons to move on. They were out for blood and didn't want to take anything less. Frannie couldn't do it though, she had to settle and get back to her life.

Hector was clearly getting better and she wanted to focus on him. She found a new long term facility to take

Hector but they couldn't get him in for a couple days so they were sending a nurse a couple times a day to check on him which took some stress off of Frannie but added more guilt. She had also been watching him closer, looking for movements but she hadn't seen any since they saw his eyes moving. She prayed constantly to whichever entity would listen to her to bring her husband back.

"Just let us be mad, okay? We know that we can't change anything but we're mad. That dirty, piece of garbage man is just walking free. He gets to live his life, we got ours stolen!" Angelo walked out of the room, his hand through his hair like he was trying to pull it out, Dominic followed close behind.

"Where are you going? Angelo! Dominic!" Gianna ran to the doorway, watching them as they approached the front door.

"To get a drink. Want to come or you going to yell at us about that too?" and with that, Angelo and Dominic were out the door with a slam.

"Gianna, give them time. This is hard on everyone." Frannie got up and crossed the kitchen to her daughter. She could see that Gianna was close to a breakdown and she hugged her. "They will be fine. They just need time to process all of this. It's...a lot to process."

"I know, but acting like Neanderthals won't help that, Mom. It's only going to hurt the rest of us who are trying to heal. And, really? Going to drink in the middle of the day seems like a bad idea to me..."

"I know but we all are going to handle this differently. Let them be mad, let them go. Just work on you, work on getting yourself through this." Frannie pulled away from the hug and smiled at her daughter. She wanted to take her own advice and get herself through this but she knew it was a long road.

"Okay, Mom. Are you going to be okay?"

"Of course I am. The settlement wasn't really that bad. I mean, yeah they aren't claiming any responsibility but the amount of money we're getting from it is insane. I really can't even wrap my head around it..." Frannie looked over at

Paul who was still sitting at the kitchen table. He gave her a reassuring smile and she smiled back.

Paul had been Frannie's silent partner in all of this chaos. He was fully on Hector and Frannie's side but he would be lying is he said he didn't feel conflicted at the trial. He had worked for that company for over 30 years and now it felt as if he were turning his back on them even though he knew what they had done was incredibly wrong. He felt an enormous amount of guilt when he was watching Hector's children deal with the accident because he still blamed himself. He knew he couldn't have stopped the accident from happening but he also knew that he had to move past that. He couldn't continue to beat himself up over something that happened. He was a good supervisor and he knew that. This was something that had been purposely hidden from him and covered up without his knowledge. He had to keep reminding himself that he was not to blame.

Gianna looked over at the digital clock on the stove and started collecting her things, "I have to go get Bobby from school. Call me if you need help, Mom, for real. I'll be over quick. You can call the guys too, they'll help, but maybe not tonight, I'm sure they're going to feel awful tomorrow too, but after that, they'll help." Frannie smiled at her daughter and gave her a kiss on the cheek before Gianna ran out of the house.

Paul watched Frannie as she opened the fridge door and pulled out two cans of diet Pepsi, offering one to him. "Thanks. So…what are you going to do with all that money? How do you feel about it?"

"Well…I know I need some sort of advisor. It's too much money for me to know what to do with, but a lot of it is going to go into savings. I'm not sure really what I'll do aside from that. I…don't really know what to think about it. I don't feel like we deserve *that* much but I don't know if Hector will ever work again, so I guess it makes sense." She started walking into the living room; Paul stood up and followed her.

"You definitely deserve it, Fran. Your whole family has been through so much. This is just a small piece of what they should be doing for you. Think about the amount of money Hector would be getting every year until he retired. Believe me, this is the least they could do…for real." They both sat on the sofa and Frannie leaned her head back against it, taking a deep breath and closing her eyes for a moment.

"I want to open up savings accounts for all the kids. Hector always wanted to make sure that none of them would have to struggle. I always thought it was a pipe dream, I never thought we'd actually be able to help them like this, but we can now, so I want to make sure all the grandkids are set for college. I don't want them to struggle like we did when we were young. I want to give some to my kids, give them enough to let them relax a bit. They all work so hard for their families. Gianna is a single mom with a house but she's never asked for help and Angelo has his whole family to take care of. Dominic…he's been such a help with Hector and I know it wasn't easy to move back to Michigan after living in New York. He gave up his job to come be with his dad."

"Those all sound like great ideas, Frannie. Hector always talked to me about putting money away for your kids. I think this is something he would definitely want." Paul thought back to different conversations that he'd had with Hector at work. Hector had always worried about his family and how his children would live lives that he never had at their ages. He remembered the stories Hector would tell him about struggling to have a wedding or pay for his sons to play in little league or for Gianna to compete in dance.

"I can't believe that we're able to do that now, though. Just the thought of my kids and grandkids not having to struggle…it's a lot to process." Frannie sat up, pulled her legs up onto the couch and looked at Paul, "You know what else I can't really believe? That Frank got probation…that's it. He agreed to a 12-step program and probation? That just blows my mind." Frannie felt as if she could let her real feelings out now that her children were gone. She agreed with all of them in different ways but she didn't feel as if the punishment fit the crime. "I know it sounds bad but where is the jail time? I understand that he doesn't have a record but that doesn't change anything. That doesn't change that it happened and that Hector is now lying in there for who knows how much longer?" She waved her hand toward the dining room.

"You're right about all of that. It's not fair, but that's what happened. He took a deal to testify against the lawyer and because of that, he got a smaller sentence. None of this situation is fair, Frannie, but you've done an amazing job keeping it together so far. This was the end of it. Now all you have to focus on is Hector and dealing with your loads of cash now." Paul joked with Frannie, hoping to keep the mood light.

Frannie smiled at Paul then took a drink of her diet Pepsi, her mind swirling with the possibilities of this money. She knew that she was going to start a savings account for her children and her grandchildren. She knew she was going to be responsible and put a lot of the money away but she wanted to do one fun thing with the money. "What if when Hector wakes up, we take everyone on vacation? Something to celebrate his life and a chance to relax after the hardest few years of our lives? Hector is getting better every day. He's been moving his eyes; I can see them under his eyelids. He went from being on all those machines to just the monitors. That's such a big improvement. If he keeps going like this, I'd think by this time next year we could all be on a plane to somewhere tropical, don't you think?"

"Hector was moving his eyes? You saw them?" Paul wanted to be as optimistic as Frannie but he couldn't.

Situations like Hector's never can be predictable but he also didn't want to ruin her mood.

"Yes! How did I not tell you?! The other night, after you left, I went in his room and under his eyelids I saw his eyes rolling around. I think he heard me though, when I came in because they stopped when I yelled for Dominic. I've been watching them since but I haven't seen anything. Paul, I truly think he's getting better. These all seem like good signs to me."

For the first time in a while, Paul saw Frannie really smile. She seemed genuinely happy in this moment, thinking about what kind of vacation she and Hector would be taking everyone on. The excitement in her eyes gave Paul the hope he wanted when it came to Hector but the reality of the situation washed over him as he looked at the equipment and bed that had now taken up permanent residence in the dining room. He quickly turned back to Frannie with a smile, watching as she went on, unrealistically in Paul's mind, about this fantasy trip they were going to take. "That sounds like a perfect plan. I know Hector would love to do something like that."

"I can only be grateful that we are going to be able to do something like that. We struggled, not awfully, but still struggled most of our lives. I remember feeling as if I was skating through life and I'm not a good skater. I was barely staying upright, but now I won't have to worry about that. I'm going to keep working for now, until Hector wakes up. Then when he does, every minute will be spent with him. I love that I have the option to not work, though, unlike the people that were fired. I do feel bad about that. Not about Frank, but I know a couple other people lost their jobs due to this case. I'm sure people that didn't have really anything to do with it will lose their jobs…" As Frannie said this, it dawned on her that the man sitting next to her was the Supervisor on duty when the accident happened. She looked over at Paul, who was looking down at his soda can. "Oh Paul, were you one of them?"

All Paul could do was look up at Frannie with a plastered-on smile and nod. He had been told a few days ago that he would be terminated without any sort of compensation and had no idea how to let her know.

"Paul…I never meant for you to lose your job…I hope you know that…" Frannie sat up straight, looking over at Paul, a worried look on her face.

"Oh, I know. Frannie, believe me, it's okay. I'll be okay. I had a feeling this was going to happen, especially after everything was covered up. It really only made sense that the supervisor on duty wouldn't have a job anymore. I'm honestly surprised it took this long to happen. I'll be just fine. I'll find another job."

"We can help you with anything you need; it's truly not a problem. There is enough for all of us to live off of so please, do not ever hesitate to ask for help. You are our family too." Frannie reached out and put a hand over Paul's, giving it a squeeze. "Please, let me know if you need anything. Anything, Paul."

Paul felt tears welling up in his eyes as he looked across the sofa to a woman that he knew as his friend but who was slowly becoming his family. A woman that had gone to hell and back in the last few years was sitting across from him, offering help for the very accident that sent her there.

For the first time since the trial, Paul opened up to Frannie and let his tears fall. He wasn't worried about looking weak, he wasn't ashamed for crying and he knew that with Frannie, he was safe. He was able to feel his emotions and express them to someone who completely understood him. He felt Frannie wrap her arms around him as he cried. "Frannie, you should not be the one offering me help. I should be helping you...I should be here for you..."

"Paul, you lost a friend too and even though he's just a room over, it's not the same and I understand that. This whole situation is one big mess and all we can ask of ourselves is to keep going so when Hector does come back, we're here for him. That's all we can do, be here for him and each other. You've been such a big help these last few weeks with the trial and I know I can count on you. Thank you for being here for my family, Paul." Frannie didn't know how long it had been since they sat down to talk but when she glanced out the sliding glass door, she noticed how dark it had gotten. "Do you want to go sit outside on the back porch and get some fresh air? We may be able to see some nice stars out there."

Paul smiled at Frannie, wiping his eyes on his sleeve and nodded. "I'd like that. I used to sit out there with Hector a lot, he'd start a fire and we'd talk about…anything really." He stood up and as they were getting ready to walk out the door, Frannie's landline started to ring.

"You go out, I'll grab us another pop after I get this, okay?" Frannie walked over to the phone and picked up the receiver, cradling it between her shoulder and ear as she went to the fridge to pull out more drinks. "Hello?"

"Mrs. Plata? This is Officer Darren Bolts from the Wayne Police Department. We've got Dominic Plata here at the station and the man with him says that they are your sons. Is that correct?"

"Yes. Dominic and Angelo. Is everything okay?" Frannie felt the dread in her chest starting to push outwards. She couldn't handle another accident, especially if it involved her sons. Her mind was starting to blur and she felt like she could hardly make a sentence.

"Something is wrong with the boys? Frannie, what's wrong with our boys?"

Hector had been listening to the arguing between his children earlier that day and the soft conversation between Frannie and Paul all afternoon, barely being able to make out what they were saying but with Frannie only one room over, he could hear her voice crystal clear. He could tell by the tremble in her words that something had happened and he felt his body responding. The hairs on his arms started to stand up, his heart started beating harder and he felt the sweat starting to form on his forehead.

"Frannie, go get our boys. Make sure they're safe."

Paul watched Frannie from the sliding glass door and recognized the panic on her face. He went over to her in the kitchen and watched as she stood still, her breath coming in short bursts. "Frannie, is everything okay? It's the boys? What's wrong with them?"

"Everything is fine, Mrs. Plata, we just need someone to come pick them up. We can discuss the details when you're here."

"Of course. I'm on my way right now." Frannie hung up the phone and looked over at Paul, wanting to ask him if he'd go with her but he beat her to the punch.

"I'll drive. Where are we going?"

During the entire trip to the police station all Frannie could do was to try to calm her mind. The police officer had said that everyone was all right, but the boys were there so something had to have happened. She knew they truly had to be all right; otherwise, she would be getting a call from the hospital and not the police station. Paul pulled into the parking lot and had barely put the car in park before Frannie had jumped out and headed for the door. She was stopped in the vestibule when the door was locked but heard a buzz and a woman's voice asking why she was there. Frannie explained who she was and that she had just gotten a phone call and was here to pick up her sons.

She walked up to the woman at the front desk after being let in, looking around for her sons but not seeing them. "Hi. I was called by…Officer Books…or eh, it started with a B."

"Bolts. Mrs. Plata? Nice to meet you, I'm Officer Bolts." Frannie turned around and found a squat man holding his hand out for her. His face was red and although his bulbous nose was the center of attention, she could tell from the pockmarks that he had struggled with acne. She shook his hand and continued to look for her boys when Paul walked in after going through the security labyrinth, catching up with her. "Ah, this must be your husband? Hello, Mr. Plata."

Paul looked down at Frannie then back up at the officer. "No, Sorry, just a family friend. Are the boys okay?"

"Yes, they're fine. Just sobering up. They're through here, follow me."

Frannie looked up at Paul and mouthed "Sorry." He shook his head and smiled at her. They followed the officer through a door into the back of the police station where they saw both Angelo and Dominic lying across benches, behind bars. Dominic shot up and stumbled a little but Angelo didn't move. Frannie walked over to the bar and shook her head. "Dom...what happened...? Is he okay?"

"Yep, we's a both good. We eh, just drank some too much, okay?" Frannie stepped back, smelling the alcohol on her son's breath. She patted his hand on the bar and joined Officer Bolts and Paul.

"What happened? Did they get into a fight?"

"No, well...no, not technically in a fight with anyone...just...with themselves? They didn't fight each other, they kind of...well, I don't actually know, they just were hitting themselves. It concerned a few people at the bar they were at and we were called. We got them to come with us in the car so that's the only reason they are here. They've been very polite, actually."

Frannie sighed and hung her head for a moment then looked back up. "So we can just take them home? They weren't actually arrested?"

"Correct. We ran a background on both of them and they're clean so this just looks like a bad night to me, no need to actually arrest them. They cooperated with us too, so they're good. They did keep saying something about their dad? I assumed it was you," He looked over at Paul, "but I see now that isn't the case. If you don't mind me asking, ma'am, did something happen with their dad?"

"Yes, we went to court today for him. He was in an accident a few years back at work, some car parts fell on him and he's been in a coma ever since. Anyway, we got the verdict about what was going to happen to the man that caused the accident and the boys weren't really happy about it so I can only imagine that's why they were like this." Frannie began to stand up when the officer started talking again.

"Plata...you're talking about the man from the car plant? He lived? I thought for sure he wasn't going to survive that." The officer stood and shook both Frannie and Paul's hand.

"Yes, he survived, barely. He was on machines up until a few weeks ago, he's breathing on his own now but he's still in the coma. We're all holding out hope that he'll get better soon."

"Of course, ma'am. We'll be thinking about him. I had no idea he was still alive. I remember hearing about it, though, I didn't go on the call but I definitely heard about it." He walked over to the cell and opened it up. Dominic walked out but Angelo stayed on the bench. Frannie took a few steps towards him then stopped abruptly as Angelo sat up and vomited all over the cell floor. She jumped back and looked over at the officer with wide eyes. He just waved her off and radioed for clean-up. Paul walked around the mess, put his arm under Angelo and helped him walk, grabbing a trash bag from one of the janitors that had shoved it towards him, scowling at the mess.

"Hi, Mom! I just threw up…and it came out my nose…" Frannie gave a tight smile at her inebriated son and headed towards the car, grateful that she only lived a few minutes away.

Chapter 11

Hector couldn't take it anymore. He couldn't take being the burden on his family and he couldn't take the stress that he was constantly feeling. He wanted to be up with his family, he wanted to feel like he was actually there, not just a decoration in the dining room.

While Frannie and Paul had gone out to retrieve the boys from their drunken escapades, Hector felt helpless. This was a feeling that he had experienced many times in recent years but hearing that something was wrong with his kids and not being able to be there for them or his wife pushed him further into the darkness that was his mind at that moment. He had been listening to the complaining and the yelling. He had heard how much his family was still struggling with the outcome of the trial and he knew that while it would hurt a lot, his family would eventually get over him if he would just pass away already. He felt that by still being alive and in this coma all he was doing was stringing his family along. He wanted to get better, he worked at getting better every day, but the enormous amount of effort it took him to do simple things like twitch his finger or roll his eyes up was enough to exhaust him. His heart couldn't take it and while he felt his days coming to an end, no one else did.

Hector had accepted that his days were numbered and he almost felt the weight lift off of his chest. The amount of physical pain his body was in constantly and the mental stress of his situation had come to a head and had taken over his thoughts. The Cuckoo clock that had been a sense of familiarity and calming had turned into the same repetitive mocking that any clock had become. A constant reminder that everyone else was living their lives and he spent every moment of his confined to a bed, unable to have a conversation with anyone but himself and a burden to his family. He stopped keeping track of the time now and even if it was day or night. He knew when people were around him and when they were not. He knew when he was in pain and when he wasn't, which was starting to be less and less. The pain his muscles were starting to feel and the amount of energy it took him to just be coherent was wearing on his mind. The proverbial light at the end of the tunnel was getting bigger and while Hector knew he was close to waking up, he also knew he was closer to never waking up again. He just needed to get better before he couldn't anymore.

Only a few things brought Hector any sort of peace during his otherwise empty days and most of those things involved his grandsons. He loved when he would hear the little yells coming up the front steps and the shoes of tiny feet being kicked into the walls like he had today. He braced himself for the two little boys to climb up on his bed to play with him. While they never made much sense, he still loved hearing their little conversations and that they felt comfortable enough to be with him. He was happy that everyone else in the house allowed them to be on his bed. Frannie had tried to stop them in the beginning, but after she saw how nicely they played and she wanted them to have memories with their grandfather, so she stopped.

He felt the little hands pulling at his blankets, climbing up and the little voices talking to each other, Leaf a little clearer than Buzz and like every other time, he felt the little wheels of cars driving over his body like cars driving through a mountain range.

"Hey, little buddies! You're back to play with grampa! What cars do you have today? The bulldozer or maybe the big school bus?"

While some days the pain of the cars would be excruciating, there was nothing Hector could or wanted to do about it. He would have been in pain every day just to know that his grandsons were happy and able to play with their grampa.

He could hear Sage in the kitchen talking with Frannie about Angelo and her concerns. It was hard to pay attention to both the kids and the adults but Hector could make out a few pieces of the conversation. "…drinking himself..." "…can't get over it…" "…all he talks about…" He couldn't piece all the words together over the vrooms and engine noises coming from the boys but it was enough for him to know that something was wrong with Angelo. He knew that he had been really upset over how the trial ended and he knew about the minimal jail time the night before. Hector had been upset to hear about the boys, but also impressed that even while intoxicated; they were polite and gave the officers no trouble.

After what seemed like only minutes had passed, Hector heard Sage calling for her sons, telling them it was time to go. Hector had no idea how long it had actually been but he wanted to beg Sage to let them stay just a while longer. Being with his grandkids kept Hector from slipping down into a dark place. He wanted what was left of his life to be spent with his family.

Frannie walked over to Hector after kissing the boys goodbye and sat at the edge of his bed, her head in her hands. Hector could feel the tension and the stress emanating from his wife. He desperately wanted to let her know that he was there and wished he could give her the hug she needed but he wasn't strong enough to will his body to do anything right after the boys had left. It took so much energy to withstand the pressure and pain from the kids that he was left drained of energy.

"Angelo is not okay. Sage just told me that when we dropped him off last night that he went into the kitchen and started drinking again. She said that he hasn't stopped talking about Frank and what happened, that he won't let it go."

"Frannie, he's upset. He just needs a few days to wallow then he should be fine. I definitely think Frank got off easy and I'd probably be doing the same thing, except that I can't. He will be fine, honey, I promise."

"I just hope he'll be fine. I'm going to give him a few days before I get involved. He needs to process all this, I just hope he doesn't destroy himself in the meantime…" Frannie put her hands out in front of her, grabbing onto Hector's arm and took a deep breath. "We will all be fine. This is all just…a blip in our lives. You'll be awake soon…"

"Frannie, please…stop getting your hopes up. I want to wake up, baby, I do, but I don't want to disappoint you. If I could just hold you one more time, my life will be great. You all need to move on, and it's hard to do that with me looming over you. Please just focus on yourself and our kids…not me anymore, I will be fine."

Hector felt as if the life was being sucked out of him. He needed to see his wife one more time but he knew not to try opening his eyes right now. He knew that he would have to save his energy and his strength for a time when he really needed it, so he slipped off to sleep.

Frannie closed her eyes and leaned forward, resting her forehead against Hector's arm. "Please, please, please Hector. I need your help. I need to know what to do with Angelo. I need your help..." Frannie whispered as she started to cry. She cried for her son and she cried for herself. She felt alone in the world right now and all she wanted was her husband by her side. Frannie had been strong for two years, breaking down only by herself but the weight of the situation had caused her to snap. She had been so distracted by her racing thoughts that she hadn't heard the door open and didn't hear the footsteps coming towards her. She only sat up when she heard Derrick's voice.

"Ma, are you okay? Did something happen? Is Hector okay?" He took a few fast steps and was on Hector's other side, checking the screens of the monitors and making sure everything was hooked up.

"Yes, I'm okay, I'm sorry." Frannie wiped the tears from her cheeks with her sleeve. "There's just a lot going on right now...Where's Dominic?"

"He's grabbing a few things from the car. I came in to start prepping for dinner. I wanted to make something for everyone. Do you think Angelo and Gianna will come over? I think maybe we all just need to do something normal and familiar and what we're used to." Once Derrick was sure Hector was okay, he looked down at Frannie. "Do you need me to get you something? Anything? I don't want you to worry about cooking; Dom and I have it tonight."

Frannie smiled and shook her head. "I can call the other kids, see if they want to come over. I think Gianna was bringing Bobby over tonight anyway. Sage was just here, she said Angelo's not doing too well so I wouldn't be surprised if they pass on tonight." Frannie got up to call Angelo but only got his voicemail. "I'll text him, maybe he'll see that instead."

Dominic walked in the door with a handful of bags. Frannie could see fresh vegetables poking out and the top of a wine bottle. "Mom, we're going to cook dinner tonight, ok?"

"I know, thank you. Derrick told me not to help."

"Well…I mean…you could help, but you don't have to. I can kind of, sort of cook a little bit." Dominic looked up at Frannie with a look she can only describe as his awkwardly overwhelmed face.

"Nope. No help. We're going to do this. I'm going to teach you how to cook, tonight is the night!" Derrick smiled and waved Frannie out of the kitchen just as Gianna and Bobby came through the front door.

"Gramma! At school we got to play with the building blocks and I made a big tower of the red ones but my friend Rory knocked it down and I was mad but I didn't hit him, I just told him that wasn't nice and I walked away from him then I went to the table to color a picture and the teacher told me that we were drawing a picture of our family and I drewed this!" Bobby shoved a picture up to Frannie that made her want to go back to crying on Hector. The picture Bobby drew consisted of 7 tall stick figures, one for each adult in the family, all labeled with arrows above their heads, 1 medium sized stick figure labeled "Me" above it and two short stick figures for his younger cousins. On the end of the bunch, Bobby drew a bed with a stick figure in it and "Grampa" next to the arrow. Frannie felt her face fall and instantly put on a smile.

"Bobby, my love, this is fantastic! You got everyone in there!" Frannie looked up at her daughter who obviously was thinking the same thing Frannie was.

"Gramma, I drewed the babies and me and all the 'dults. I even put grampa in there, see!" Bobby pointed to his picture, a smile on his face. "The teacher told us that we could write a story about our family too. I brought it with me, you want to hear it? It's all about us, Gramma!" Bobby was so excited about his picture and story that he didn't even wait to hear her answer. He pulled the story from his backpack, ran into the room with Hector and jumped up on his bed, right next to Hector's head. Frannie followed him into the dining room and sat at the end of the bed, rubbing his leg with her hand.

Feeling his bed shift, Hector woke up and instantly heard his oldest grandson talking and the rustle of paper right next to his ear. He loved when Bobby came to visit because he was always so aware of Hector and what was going on. It was nice to have someone talk to him and have a normal conversation, not that he didn't like when Frannie talked to him. When Frannie talked to him, Hector felt overwhelmed and guilty through no fault of Frannie's but when Bobby talked to him, Hector didn't feel any of that. It didn't feel like Hector was letting Bobby down by not being awake, Bobby just took it for what it was and didn't know the difference.

"I wanted Grampa to hear it too, so I camed in here. He's in it Gramma! 'Member when he teached me about getting the silver from the dirt? Member, he said that my name means silver? Member that, Gramma?"

"I do, buddy. I remember that story you're talking about. Your Grampa loved to tell that to you, huh?" Frannie was trying to prepare herself for Bobby's story, not really sure what to expect from it. "Go ahead and read me your story, Grampa is listening too."

"Oh, a story! Let's hear it, Bobby, I bet it's fantastic!"

Bobby began reading in short bursts and pauses between each word as he flipped open the book to the first page, a picture with the two younger boys on it. "These are not my brothers. This is Buzz like Buzz Lightyear and this is Leaf like the tree. They have weird names but they are pretty awesome. I like to play trucks and cars with them and eat ice cream from the ice cream man." Frannie smiled down at her grandson as he flipped to the next page. "This is my Mommy. She is a good mommy and doesn't yell at me all the time, just sometimes." Frannie let out a laugh which made Bobby laugh too. "That was funny? Gramma, that was funny!"

Gianna poked her head out of the kitchen and gave Bobby a playfully mad look and he gave it right back. Just at that moment, a crash came from the kitchen and some words flew from Dominic's mouth that Bobby shouldn't have heard. Gianna and Frannie both whipped around to see what happened. Frannie turned back to her grandson and told him, "I'm sorry buddy, I have to go see what happened. You keep reading to Grampa and we'll finish the story later, okay?"

Bobby nodded as she walked out of the room but wasn't really paying attention to her; he had already continued to read his story to Hector, who was enjoying every minute.

"These are my uncles Dominic and Derrick. They aren't married but my mommy says that they can be if they want to be. They love each other though and they kiss each other."

"Oh boy, how do you explain that to a room full of 6-year-olds? At least he gets it."

Hector loved that Bobby had some diversity in his life but he knew that not everyone had the same experiences that Bobby had and some might not understand the relationship that Derrick and Dominic had.

"This is my Uncle Angelo and Aunt Sage. Buzz and Leaf have them as mommy and daddy. My Aunt Sage likes to put weird stuffs on my body in the summer. She said that it is better than sunscream." Bobby flipped the page to a picture drawn of Frannie. "This is my Gramma, I love her a lot. She is my best friend. My Gramma always has hugs and kisses for me, even when she is sad." He flipped to the next page of his story, a picture of him and Hector in the back yard. He pointed to Hector on the page, "That's you, Grampa! 'Member you used to walk? You 'member that?"

Hector wanted to tell his grandson that he did remember that. He remembered running around the backyard with him and he remembered going for walks, pushing the handle on the toddler bike he used to have. This was the first time that Bobby had said he remembered his Grampa outside of a hospital bed.

"Oh...this is going to be rough..."

"My Grampa is a part of my family, too. He teached me to dig. He told me that silver is in the ground. You have to dig for it." Bobby looked over at Hector. "'Member you said to me that the silver is sleeping underground, it silen' until someone finds it and wakes it up."

Hector chuckled to himself. *"Silent buddy, there's a T. The silver is silent until its awakened."*

"My Grampa told me that my name means silver in Spanish. Plata is Spanish for silver. You can dig plata from the ground."

"Very good, buddy! You're right. I'm very impressed, Bobby." Hector heard the next page turn and was waiting to hear some other piece of wisdom he had taught Bobby but instead, he felt the weight of the world as this 6-year-old read from his story that he wrote about his family.

"My Grampa doesn't walk anymore. He was in a accident at his car work and now he just sleeps all day. I miss my Grampa a lot. I want him to wake up so he can play with me again." A page flipped and Hector hoped for a lighter one. "My grampa could wiggle his ears and he trieded to teach me to but I can't do it. He needs to wake up so he can teached me how to wiggle my ears."

Hector could hear the sadness in Bobby's voice and the trembling of his lip as he spoke about him.

"Oh Bobby, buddy, I'm right here with you. I can hear you and I'm sorry I can't teach you to wiggle your ears anymore. You were getting so close, buddy! Damn it! I can't handle this anymore. Bobby, look at me buddy, see my ears?"

Hector summoned any strength he could, needing to show his grandson that he heard him, needing him to believe that his Grampa was still there. He focused all his energy on his ears, he pulled strength he didn't know he had, willing the muscles to move, just enough for Bobby to see it. He knew the book was right by his ear so he hoped that Bobby would notice them moving and understand that he was listening to him. Hector felt his body begin to weaken but he pushed through it, his heart starting to race and beat harder but he finally felt it. He felt his ears moving, wiggling as they did before his accident, before he abandoned his family and before he was nobody. It was less than 10 seconds but he knew that Bobby had seen them by the way he stopped reading.

"Gramma! Mom! His ears! They moved! Mom! Grampa's ears moved!" Gianna came running into the dining room after hearing her son yelling and looked him over, not really hearing what he had been saying.

"What's wrong, buddy?"

"Mom! Grampa moved his ears! 'Member how he wiggled them for us? He just did that! He did!" Gianna looked down at her dad and up at the monitor's screen right as the alarms started to go off. She picked Bobby up off the bed and pushed him towards the door. "But his ears moved, Mom! His ears moved!"

"Buddy, go in the other room, okay?" Bobby looked at his mom and watched as the rest of the adults ran into the room, his Gramma running to his Grampa's side and checking all the monitors.

Frannie looked down at Hector, scanning his body for a misplaced monitor but not finding one. She put her fingers on his wrist, checking his pulse. "Gianna, call an ambulance, his heart rate is through the roof."

Gianna ran from the room on her cell phone and Frannie tried to think of anything she could do to help Hector. "Calm down baby, calm down. Slow your heart down, stay with me, and calm down." She wiped his forehead with the sheet and uncovered him. He had begun to sweat now and Frannie knew that wasn't a good sign. Dominic and Derrick were standing in the doorway to the kitchen when they looked over and saw Bobby watching all of this happen. They swooped down and grabbed him, taking him into the other room so he wouldn't see anything he shouldn't.

"Uncle Dom, did you see his ears move? He wiggled them like he used to! He wiggled them for me right as I was reading the part in my story about him teaching me to wiggle my ears! Did you see them?!" Bobby was trying to push his uncle off of him to get back to his grampa but being small had its disadvantages.

"Frannie, baby...I'm so sorry...I just...I needed him to know I was here...I shouldn't have pushed it..."

Hector's body was betraying him now and shutting down. All this time he had wanted to die and now that he was steps away from it all he wanted to do was live. He wanted to hug his wife and tell his kids he loved them. He wanted to be alive and he started to regret all the time he spent wishing away his existence.

In a matter of only minutes, the EMT's were in Frannie's living room, preparing to transport Hector to the local hospital where he had originally gone when the accident happened. As they were loading him into the back of the ambulance, Frannie tried to climb up but was met with resistance.

"I'm sorry, ma'am. You can't ride in here with him. We need you to follow us."

Frannie felt her heart drop and her breath catch in her throat. "No. I'm going with him, I'm riding with him."

The EMT's looked at each other and said, "That's not how this works. We can't have you in here. We have rules and there are laws we have to follow…"

Frannie cut them off, feeling as if her world was crumbling around her and she couldn't hold back the years of fear, anger, and desperation. "I'm going with you. I don't care about the Goddamn laws! That is my husband and if he dies, he'll be dying next to me! I am getting in this ambulance and I will be riding with him, okay?!"

They saw the rage in Frannie's eyes and decided that this wasn't a fight they were going to win anytime soon. They couldn't afford to lose another minute of Hector's life so they moved to the side, letting her in.

Frannie watched the EMT's as they tried to get Hector's heart to beat normally again. She tried to fight the dread that was seeping into her chest like it had when Hector had been in the accident but this felt different. She was right here, watching her husband struggle and there was nothing she could do. She was losing him and she knew it. She wished that he could hold her one more time, that he could look up at her with his beautiful brown eyes or that she could see his smile just once more but she felt deep in her heart that this was going to be it. She thought he was getting stronger but she saw now that she had been wrong.

Arriving at the hospital was a whirlwind of emotion. Hector was rushed into the ER and the nurses had told Frannie to stay there, she decided not to push this fight and stayed in the waiting room. Within minutes, the rest of her family had surrounded Frannie, asking for updates but she had nothing to give them.

"How is he, Mom? Where did they take him?"

"I don't know. They just took him through the doors. They were working on his heart but…it was just all so fast I don't actually know what they were doing. He started to have a seizure though…I…" Frannie looked down, trying to be strong. She thought back to a few minutes before as they were pulling into the driveway for the hospital. Even more chaos erupted from the back of the ambulance as Hector's body had started to convulse. She had watched with panic as her husband, whom she hadn't seen move more than a single muscle in two years was suddenly flailing around on a small gurney. Frannie had lunged forward, trying to be next to Hector but the woman working on Hector pushed her back into her seat. She had sat in the corner, covering her mouth and shaking.

"Sit down, Frannie." She looked up to see Paul, his hand on her shoulder, and she broke down. Without a beat, Paul wrapped her in a hug and sat her down on the chair, squeezing her tight. "I know, Fran. He'll be all right. He's already been through so much; he can get through this, too."

Frannie could only shake her head, sobbing into Paul's shoulder. "Paul, they were working on his heart, but they kept saying they weren't getting any response. Then…then he started shaking and moving, more than I've seen him move in years…"

Paul continued to rub Frannie's back as he looked around the room at all of her children. Gianna was standing across from them, crying with an arm from Dominic around her. He was grateful that she had thought to call him. Derrick was sitting a few seats from Frannie and Angelo was up at the reception desk, trying to get any information he could. Paul knew that in this moment, he had to be the strong one. He had to help hold this family together even when he wanted to break down too. He sat Frannie back in the chair and looked at her, "Frannie, we have to be strong for Hector. We have to hold onto hope, okay? I know that's a lot to ask but it's all we can do in this moment. We don't know how he is but that doesn't mean that it's bad. All we can do is wait for the doctor, okay? Do you need something to drink? Anything?"

Frannie shook her head and looked around at her children, wiping the tears from her eyes. She had her moment to break down and she knew that she had to regain her strength. She knew that she had to be there for her children.

"They said they don't have any information for us yet, that they will let us know when they can." Angelo sat down next to his mom, his elbows on his knees and his head in his hands. Frannie reached over and rubbed his back but she knew that she couldn't say anything that would help him right now. She was just happy that he was there.

The weight that had positioned itself in the bottom of Frannie's stomach continued to grow as the minutes passed. She felt regret for all the time that she spent away from

Hector, but also for the time she spent wishing the situation would be over. She knew there were moments in the past two years where she resented Hector for putting her through this. She blamed him for not being more aware of what was going on or for not getting out of the way quicker. These moments never lasted very long but they still happened and the crushing negative emotions that were taking over her body were hard to fight. She looked over at Paul, knowing that one of the kids must have called him on their way to the hospital and felt just a little bit of relief knowing that she had a friend like him to be by her side during this time. Frannie took a deep breath, trying to relax her muscles as she waited to hear if her husband was still alive.

Chapter 12

A few hours later in the ICU, Frannie looked down at her husband, his still body looked the same as it had for the last two years but this time, something was different. She had seen all his muscles move in the ambulance but she knew that wasn't of his doing. She knew that something terrible had happened to Hector and while she didn't want to accept it, she knew that this could be the end for him. Frannie let the tears drop from her eyes and roll down her swollen cheeks as she was knocked back into the moment by Angelo's hand on her back.

"Mom, did you hear her?"

Frannie wiped her face and looked back up at the tall, slim doctor. She had fair skin and long dark hair that was wrapped up in a bun high on the back of her head. "I'm sorry, I didn't hear you."

"I was saying that while Mr. Plata is stable right now, he is in very critical condition. His heart is failing and from what we can tell, it's because he's been sedentary for so long. Other muscles in his body are starting to atrophy, which just means that they are basically wasting away from not being used as they should be. One of his kidneys has completely stopped working, along with other parts of major organs and a large portion of his heart is looking to be the same way. Mrs. Plata, you have a few options here but I'm afraid none of them are as good as we'd like them to be. We can try to make him as comfortable as possible and continue to have him on life support...until you're ready to suspend further treatment. You don't have to make any decisions now, but please just know that we will do whatever we can. Please, talk it over with your family. I'd tell you to take a few days but honestly, I don't think we have that long."

Frannie nodded at the doctor, holding onto the railing of Hector's bed, feeling like if she were to let go, she might float away. He had an IV in his hand and monitors attached to his chest that hadn't been there before and he had to be hooked back up to a ventilator. Frannie wondered how long his heart had been failing and if bringing him home had made it worse.

"Please let us know if you need anything. Any of you. We know this is a hard time and we want to make it as smooth as possible." The doctor checked the screens next to the hospital bed, gave the room a trying smile and left.

"Mom, what are you thinking right now?" Angelo put his hand on Frannie's arm, trying to guide her to a chair but she wouldn't move. She continued to look down at Hector, desperately trying to figure out what he would have wanted. She pulled her arm away from Angelo and placed her hand lightly on Hector's chest, wanting to feel his heartbeat. She could barely feel the thumping under his pale skin; something that gave her a little bit of relief to know that he was still alive but also threw her mind into confusion and grief. She knew that Hector was never going to wake up now and as bad as she felt about it, she almost wished that his heart would stop on its own so she didn't have to make this decision. The doctor had made it clear that Hector wouldn't come back but she didn't know how long she was actually going to have with him.

"I don't know. I thought he was getting better…and the whole time he was just getting worse. I know I've seen him move, though. I saw him move his eyes and didn't Bobby say he was wiggling his ears? Of all things, why would his ears just wiggle on their own?"

"Mom, it's Bobby, he's 6. He could have hit Dad's ear with the book and thought it wiggled." Gianna walked up by her mom now, looking down at her dad. "And if they really did wiggle, then it could have just been a coincidence. Mom, he's been gone a long time, do we really want to keep this going? What if he's in pain? His organs are shutting down…"

"Really? Your response to all this is just 'Pull the plug!' Seriously, Gianna, you're that ready for him to be gone?" Angelo was staring daggers at his sister.

"Angelo, please. You have to think of the bigger picture! Is this really a life for someone? Do you want dad to just continue to lie in the bed with all his organs shutting down? Or would you like him to get some peace?" Gianna had tears rolling down her face but she kept herself very composed. Dominic sat against the windowsill, silent but completely aware of the decision that had to be made and Paul stood by the door, watching as this family had to make the hardest decision of their lives. Derrick had gone home to help Sage out with the children.

Frannie stood between the two of them, listening to the back and forth as if they were her conscience standing on her shoulders. She had struggled with these exact emotions since the beginning of Hector's new life. She knew, on one hand, at least he was alive but on the other, this was no life to be living. Frannie could keep her husband or she could give him peace. One option was selfish on her part and the other selfless. She tried to block out the noise and focus on

Hector. What would he want? What decision would he make? She slid her hand to his and laced their fingers together. His palm was no longer warm and inviting and there was no squeeze coming from his hand, nothing squeezing hers back. This body was no longer that of her husband. This was just a body now. The doctors hadn't given Hector an EEG but Frannie had known it wasn't necessary at this point. She thought that if other major organs were losing their function, his brain must have been too.

"Frannie...Oh Frannie, what happened? Why are they yelling? Why are they so loud?"

Hector was slowing coming back to consciousness. He felt Frannie squeezing his hand and he heard his children yelling about his well-being and while he appreciated their concern, all he wanted them to do was to be quiet. He knew something had happened but he wasn't sure what. His whole body felt as if he had been hit by a truck and he felt weak.

"This is it, isn't it? This is what I've been waiting for and now that it's here...Frannie, I don't want to go. I don't want to leave you but this all hurts so much. You will all be able to get closure if I am gone. I will always, always love you, Fran. I will always be watching you. You know what you need to do, right, baby? You have to let me go..."

Frannie shut her eyes to keep the tears from coming and squeezed Hector's hand again. "I need a minute." Everyone stopped and looked at Frannie.

"What? Mom, are you okay? What are you doing?" Dominic stood up and walked up to the hospital bed.

"I need to be alone with your dad. Please, give me a minute." She didn't look at anyone; she kept her eyes on Hector while everyone filed out of the room.

Paul was the last to leave but turned before he left, "Frannie, please let us know when you're ready. I know this is a hard moment, but if you're doing what I think you're doing...I support it and I support you. Come get us when you're ready."

Frannie nodded at Paul, not bothering to hide her tears anymore. She looked back down to Hector and lifted his hand to her lips, kissing it softly. "Hector...please tell me what you want me to do. Please...I can't make this decision alone..."

"Baby, please let me go. You have to let me go. My body is shutting down; I can feel it shutting down. I can feel things not working, I feel the pain. Frannie, I've been stuck in here, alone for years now and you have the ability to set me free. Fran, I wish I could tell you to let me go...I wish you could hear me..."

Hector tried to move his hand, to squeeze his fingers to let Frannie know that he was here and he was alright with the decision she needed to make. He focused his energy in the tips of his fingers but nothing moved and he felt weak.

Along with the small, soft kisses that Frannie was giving Hector's hand and fingers, tears were also landing on his skin, rolling slowly down and onto the sheets of his bed. Hector felt them falling and it reminded him of the music he created using the raindrops against the window. The only difference right now was that this song was not happy or cheerful, it was dramatic and emotional. His own personal requiem performed from the tears of his soul mate.

Frannie whispered into his hand, "I love you, so much more than I think you'll ever begin to understand. You are my life and you are my dreams. You mean everything to me, Hector, how am I supposed to make this decision? How do I decide to let you go? Please, move or blink or do something. Tell me you're here or give me some hope, please do something, baby. Please. Help me make this decision. I cannot do this alone…"

Hector continued to try to move his fingers, to give Frannie anything but he couldn't.

"You have to let go, baby, the only way to get over this is to go through it. It will be so hard and I'm so sorry that I'm doing this to you, honey, believe me, if I could take all of this back, I would. If I could go back to that day of the accident, I'd give you the best goodbye kiss I could and I'd tell you how much you mean to me and how much I love you. I never said it enough, Frannie. I never told you enough how in love I am right now and always have been with you. Ever since we were kids, it's always been you, Frannie, always. You have done so much for me and given up so much in the last two years that it's time you take your life back and if that means letting mine go, then so be it. You need to be you, Frannie, you need to move on without me. I will always be there for you, I promise."

Frannie placed her forehead against Hector's hand and let her tears soak the sheets. She knew what she had to do but she also knew it was going to upset her children. Gianna was on the same page but she knew that Angelo was going to have a hard time with the decision. Frannie worried about Dominic because he was so quiet but he also was levelheaded so she hoped he would understand. This was not a decision that could be voted on. Frannie had to make it on her own. "Hector, I love you so much. I know I need to do this for you. I don't want to say goodbye to you, but I will see you soon." She spent a little more time with her husband, just the two of them, before she stood up and walked to the door. She felt her legs shaking and her heart racing but in her gut, she knew she was making the right decision. She walked up to Paul and asked him if he could grab the doctor while she talked to her children in the hallway.

With tears and a tremble in her voice, Frannie looked at her three kids, all their eyes glued onto her, waiting on every moment that passed before she said "I know you don't want to hear this, but the best thing we can do for him is to let him go. He is struggling and I'm sure in pain, it is not fair for us to keep him going like this. He needs to be set free."

Gianna and Dominic grabbed onto each other, their sobs coming in unison while Angelo, never blinking and glaring at Frannie as tears streamed down both his cheeks, clenched his jaw and shook his head. He didn't say anything before he turned away and walked down the hallway. Frannie wanted to go after him but she didn't have the energy. Paul turned the corner just in time for Angelo to storm past him. He looked at Frannie then turned back to be with Angelo.

"I am so sorry…" Frannie's voice caught in her throat, "I know this is hard, but we have to do this for him. Please, go in and tell him goodbye…" Frannie couldn't finish her sentence as her own tears took over. She cried for herself, for preparing to lose her husband but she cried even harder for her children that were about to lose their father. She stayed in the hallway while they made their way into Hector's room. She wanted to give them privacy as they had given her. Frannie leaned against the wall outside and had her hands covering her face when she felt a hand on her shoulder, she looked up and saw the doctor.

"Your friend let me know that you made a decision about Mr. Plata's care? Is that right?"

Frannie nodded and wiped her face. "Yes…I don't think we can keep this going…if he's in pain…and his organs are failing…I can't force him to stay here with us. He's not living a life. I thought he was getting better, I thought he was starting to move but…I guess I was wrong…"

"You're making the decision you think is best for your family and that's all you can do. I'll give you a little bit before we come in so you can all say goodbye. The process can take a while, so please just be prepared for that, okay? It's sometimes quick but not all the time. You'll need to sign some paperwork for this, so I'll go get that made up and I'll come back and find you?"

Frannie nodded and took a deep breath before she walked into the room with her husband and two of her children. They were both sitting on the edge of his bed, crying.

"My babies, you have been so wonderful and I couldn't have asked for a better family. I know it's my time to go, but I need you to be strong, I need you to take care of your mother. Make sure she keeps living, make sure she smiles and make sure she's happy. I am counting on you to do all of this. Where is Angelo? Is he in here too?"

Hector heard Frannie in the hallway talking to their children and while he was relieved, he was also very scared. He had dreamt and thought of the day he was going to die but he never thought of the impact it would have on his family besides giving them closure. Listening to his children tell him goodbye was breaking his heart and he wished he could wrap them in a hug and tell them that it was going to be alright.

Frannie came over to her kids and as soon as they saw her, they stood up and hugged her, holding onto their mother and crying into her shoulders. She cried along with them, holding onto her babies tight. Paul walked in and hesitantly walked over to the group.

"Frannie...? I tried to talk to him but he said he didn't want anything to do with it and to go ahead without him. I tried to tell him that he was going to regret it but...I don't know what else to do, Fran. Maybe one of you can talk to him?" Paul looked between Gianna and Dominic. "He's outside, I can't get him to come back in."

Gianna and Dominic both walked out of the room together when Frannie looked up at Paul. "Do you want a minute alone with him?"

Paul looked over at Hector, put his hand on his leg and shook his head, "No. He knows how I feel, and I know how he feels. This is your time with him."

"Don't leave, please. I had my time with him; I don't want to be alone anymore. The doctor is getting the paperwork ready, we'll sign it and I guess they just shut the machines down. This all feels so wrong, Paul, but I know this isn't fair for him anymore. He's just suffering and we're sitting by waiting for him to get better when we all know he won't..."

Paul pulled Frannie into a hug and let her cry on his shoulder. "I know, but Fran, you are doing the right thing. It's hard because its right."

"Paul, I am so happy you are able to be here for her...She needs a good friend and you are one of the best I've ever had. You're an amazing man, and one that I would love to see in my family's lives for years to come."

Frannie pulled away from Paul and moved a chair close to Hector's bed. She sat in it and held onto Hector's hand while Paul went to the spot by the windowsill. Gianna and Dominic walked back into the room and glanced from Paul to Frannie, shaking their heads.

"He said he doesn't want anything to do with this, Mom. He said he doesn't want any part of killing his father...and he doesn't want to talk to you..." Gianna started crying harder and Dominic hugged her. "Mom, why is he so hard headed? Why can't he just accept what's going on? Dad is suffering, he is dying anyway and all we're doing is prolonging that."

"Gianna I know, believe me, I know. He processes things differently but I just hope he comes around. I don't want to do this without him but we have to do this." Frannie was terrified that Angelo was going to regret not saying goodbye to his father but she knew how stubborn he could be, only because he got that from Hector.

It was only a few minutes before the doctor came in with the paperwork but the silence in the room was deafening and once again Frannie noticed how clinical everything was.

She smelled the overpowering cleaners that were used and the ticking of the clock that droned on and on. She thought back to the last time she had been in this hospital after Hector's accident. She thought about how much hope she had gained in the time in between then and now that had completely washed away.

"Mrs. Plata? Here is the paperwork for Mr. Plata. Please read over everything and sign it at the bottom. Whenever you are ready, just let us know and we'll get started."

Frannie took the paperwork from the doctor over to Gianna and Dominic, wanting them to all read it together. Once all three had read and understood what was going on, Frannie left the room, wanting to find Angelo. She walked outside the hospital doors and found him sitting on a bench. When she sat next to him, he looked over and stood up, shaking his head.

"No. I'm not doing this, Mom. I'm not helping you with this."

"Angelo...you're going to regret not saying goodbye to your dad..."

"No, Mom, I won't. I said goodbye to him a long time ago, but that doesn't mean that I agree with all this. You're willingly going to let him slip away. You're making the decision to kill him. You're making it so my kids won't have the same memories with him that I did. Remember when we went sledding and he went on his belly? Remember how he slid past us all and crashed into the tree. Well, I'm glad you do, because my kids will never get that with him. You're not only killing my dad...you're killing my best friend."

Frannie flinched at Angelo's comments but tried to stay strong, she knew he was speaking out of anger and that he would eventually calm down. "Angelo, this has been a long time coming. He is dying anyway and we're just trying to selfishly hang on. Please, come back to the room with us."

Angelo shook his head and started walking away from her. Frannie called after him but he wouldn't look. She sat outside on the bench in the dark early morning hours for a little longer before heading back into Hector's room. She knew that she had to start the process whether Angelo was there or not. Gianna and Dominic were back on the edge of Hector's bed and Paul had stayed on the windowsill.

"Has the doctor come back yet?"

"No, it's just been us here." Gianna turned to her mom then back to her dad.

Frannie went back to her chair by the side of Hector's bed and sat down. She felt exhausted and drained but she knew this was only the beginning.

"You all know that I love you very much but this will be the best thing for everyone. My body is so tired, I am ready to be let go. I am ready to feel free."

Hector was coming to peace with the decision and his fear was dissipating. He could barely breathe, even with the machine, his heart felt like a rock in his chest and every brush against his skin felt like fire burning him.

"Mrs. Plata? Are you ready?" The doctor walked in with a nurse behind her and stood right inside the door. Frannie nodded and stood up. "No, please sit down. Be comfortable. This is already hard enough." Dominic and Gianna moved from the bed to over by Paul. They were huddled together and Frannie was thankful that they had each other. She was worried about Angelo but she had to focus on her husband right now. Frannie watched as both the nurse and the doctor walked over to Hector's bed. They started to disconnect the monitors and tubes going to him. They took out all the IVs but one. "We're going to leave this IV in. It's for pain management, we don't really know what we're dealing with but we're thinking that with all of his organs shutting down, we don't want him to be in any sort of pain while he passes."

Frannie nodded at the doctor, feeling as if she couldn't breathe. Her body was shaking even though she wasn't cold and she felt that at any moment she would pass out. She had been thankful for the doctor telling her to stay seated. The nurse leaned over Hector and disconnected the trach tube that had been helping him breathe and Frannie knew that this was the piece that was going to push Hector closer to the end.

"This is happening. Frannie...I love you so much."

Hector felt a wave of euphoria and urgency wash over his body. He had to see his wife again. Hector willed his body to open his eyes. His training had to pay off now. He felt all the IVs leaving his hand and he felt the nurse removing the trach tube. This was his chance. This was the one moment he had to look up at his wife one last time and he was going to do whatever it took to do so. He felt his body shutting down and he felt his heart beating faster. As he tried harder he heard the beep of the heart monitor speed up and he knew that he only had a few seconds.

Frannie stood up over her husband as the heart monitor began to race. Something was happening and she wasn't sure what it was. Just as she was about to let go of his hand she felt it. The squeeze she had been waiting for, the sign that Hector was with her and wasn't going to leave her. She looked at his hand and saw the muscles in his fingers flex. Her eyes zeroed in on the muscles and she called out to the doctor, "His hand is moving! Look, his hand!" She looked up at his face and saw his eyes open. His beautiful big brown eyes were looking deep into her soul. Her heart skipped a beat and she felt every nerve ending in her skin prickle. "Hector! Hector, Honey, you're back!" Frannie leaned down to him, her tears flowing freely from her eyes. The moment she has been waiting for two years was finally here. Her husband was awake and with her again. Gianna and Dominic ran over to the bed just as Angelo ran into the room. Frannie glanced over and saw Angelo's face had been red and swollen, he had been crying. None of them could believe that their dad had his eyes open. Frannie leaned down and kissed Hector's face but heard a shuddering breath escape his mouth. She looked down at him and saw his lips start to move. "Hector, what is it, baby? Tell me."

Frannie searched Hector's face for an answer then saw his beautiful smile, everything she had wanted in the last two years was finally happening. She was finally going to have her family back. After a moment and loud enough for her to hear him, he whispered "Thank you, Fran." She began to sob, overwhelmed by emotion and gratitude that her husband was with her again.

Frannie leaned over and kissed all over Hector's face, feeling his soft lips against hers just as she heard the beeping of the monitor turn into one long noise. Frannie pulled back when she realized that his lips didn't kiss her back and the sound of the monitor finally registered in her ears.

"Hector! Wait, no! Hector!" Frannie looked up at the doctor and nurse, then back at the heart monitor which had flat lined. Her joy instantly turned into grief when she realized that Hector wasn't with her anymore. She screamed for her husband, for him to come back to her. He couldn't do this to her again. She thought he was back. She saw his big eyes looking at her and she heard his voice again. There was no way that he was gone. Frannie hung onto Hector's arm as the doctor checked for a heartbeat and nurse called the time of death. Angelo ran over to his mom and wrapped her up in his arms as she fell onto the ground, her body shaking with her sobs and screams. Gianna and Dominic retreated back towards Paul as they cried, watching their hope get ripped out from in front of them. Hector had been with them again and now, he was gone.

Chapter 13

Frannie felt like a zombie, not one of those that chase after you viciously for miles, but one that just wandered aimlessly with no real purpose. She moved because she was told to and she had a hard time focusing on anything. Just a few hours before she had lived through some of the most excruciating moments of her life. After two years of waiting, Hector finally opened his eyes but as soon as they were open, they were closed again for good. Hector was awake just long enough to tell Frannie 'Thank you' and then he was gone. Frannie had been through an emotional roller coaster in a matter of a minute. She sat now in the doctor's office with her children and Paul. After they called the official time of death and pulled Frannie from the floor they had to figure out what had just happened and after two hours the doctor was confident in her findings.

"Hector had what was called Total Locked-In Syndrome. It's rare, but after consulting with a few of my colleagues I feel that this explains his last few minutes. This means that while Hector's body didn't work, his mind did. In this case, we believe it was caused by damage to his brain stem from his accident. It can also be caused by a medication overdose but with the accident causing the initial coma, that's most likely what happened here. He still heard everything, he felt everything, he just couldn't react to any of it. He had lost all function of his muscles. So that means that anytime you were talking to him, he could hear you, given that he was awake. He would have kept similar sleep patterns even though he couldn't move, and he most likely was having conversations with you, just ones that you couldn't hear."

Frannie felt every hair on her body stand up. Hector was there all along…he knew when people were around. He knew when someone was talking to him. She suddenly felt very proud that she never went a day without seeing him. She was happy that she was there for him and didn't listen to anyone when they told her that he couldn't hear her but she also felt incredibly bad for all the time he spent alone. All the time where the only thing he had was his own mind and his own thoughts. She took a deep breath when she thought about the time he'd almost drowned in his own saliva. Did he know what was going on? Her heart ached to think that he was aware of the situation and thought he was going to die.

"Everything you did for him, Mrs. Plata, he knew about. That's why we believe he said thank you right before he passed. This is truly the only explanation we could come up with for what happened. Typically with Locked-In Syndrome, the patient is able to move their eyes in a vertical motion."

"Oh my…I just saw him doing that a few days ago…I didn't know any of this. I walked in and saw his eyes moving under his eyelids. Is that what you're talking about? He was looking up and down. If we knew…could we have done anything to help him?" Frannie started to feel guilty again, wondering if she was able to help preserve his life.

"No. His organs were too far gone. Even if we knew a year and a half ago, we still really couldn't do anything. His body was not using the organs as they should have been and they were wasting away. Nothing you could have done would have saved his life, Mrs. Plata. I just want you to know that. By doing what you did, you released him from a place where he was completely alone."

Frannie felt her shoulders relax a little and she looked behind her at Angelo who was staring at the ground. She knew he would come around and even though he didn't get to really say goodbye to his father, he was there for it and that's all Frannie could have asked for.

"So, you said he couldn't move anything, but wouldn't that include his lungs too?" Gianna looked perplexed as she was trying to comprehend what the doctor was telling them.

"Yes, that would include his lungs. From his history, I see that he had been on a ventilator for a while, and then one day just stopped?"

Frannie nodded. "Yes, the facility he was in didn't attach it again after cleaning out the opening and we realized that he could breathe on his own. It was a stupid mistake but because of it Hector came home. He's been home the past couple of weeks."

"We think that was his body starting to unlock if that makes sense. There have been cases where people come out of Locked-In Syndrome and there isn't really any sort of protocol to the amount of time it takes to come out because it's been so rare. Mr. Plata's brain stem could have been recovering but because all of his organs were shutting down, this was keeping him from fully waking up."

Frannie stared at the doctor as her words flew out of her mouth, trying to piece together everything she could. She tried to remember if there were signs of Hector being awake beside his eyes moving. She tried to think back over the past two years but came up with nothing. Not until she thought of a few minutes before Hector had to be taken back to the hospital.

"His ears," Frannie looked over at Gianna, "Bobby said that his ears were wiggling right before his heart went haywire. If Hector had heard Bobby talking about his family, and that was something they used to do together...is it possible that that was Hector trying to tell Bobby that he was there and listening to him...? We didn't believe him, we didn't think anything actually happened..." Frannie looked back over to the doctor.

"That's totally possible. If his body was recovering enough to breathe on its own, I can only imagine that other muscles could have started responding as well. You said it happened right before his cardiac arrest? It's plausible that the energy it took for him to wiggle his ears would have worked his heart a little too hard. It makes sense to me, but this is such a rare thing that we really don't have all the answers and I apologize for that. I can tell you though; Hector was with you for the last two years."

Frannie bit her lip and let the tears fall from her eyes. She was happy that even if Hector hadn't been physically there, he had been mentally there. It made her feel good that she was able to keep him company in a world that he was completely alone. She thought about what it would be like to never be able to speak to anyone but you could hear them all. She thought about the solitude of being in your mind by yourself and she knew that the last two years were probably hell for Hector.

"Was he in pain? Could he feel what was happening to his body?" Angelo spoke up from the back of the room.

"That…we're not sure on. It's possible that he was in pain. To get to the point where an organ will atrophy is a very painful process but it's hard to know what he could and couldn't feel. It all really depends on the severity of the damage to his brain stem. I would venture to say that if he was starting to move again that the damage was probably minimal but enough to do what it did, obviously. The biggest thing to remember right now though, is that he is no longer in pain. You set him free, you let his mind out. Does anyone have any more questions? I promise to do my best to answer them."

Frannie looked around her, waiting for more questions to come but they didn't. She looked back over to the doctor and shook her head. "I don't think we do now. I'm sure some will pop up eventually. Thank you." They all got up and walked out of the office and down the hallway in silence.

Once they were outside, Frannie stopped and looked up at the morning sky. It had been hours since they arrived and a new day had started. It was dark and gloomy, there was thunder off in the distance and the rain was just starting. It was a late summer storm in Michigan and while Frannie thought about how stereotypical this day was, she was thankful for it. This is exactly the type of weather that Hector loved. She imagined him running around their front yard with their children and playing in the mud. She thought of the life they had together and all that they accomplished.

The others had noticed that Frannie was no longer walking with them and they stopped, looking back at her. She closed her eyes, felt the warm raindrops sprinkling her face, mixing with her tears and thought of her husband. She thought of his smile and his eyes that were always so full of life, even when she just saw them. She felt the pressure on her hand from where he had squeezed it and she thought of his last words to her. "Thank you, Fran." She felt as if she had set Hector free. Her tears felt like they would never stop but she knew right now that these tears were happy tears. Happy tears for her husband, Hector Plata, who would never have to be silenced again.

About the Authors

Carl Joseph Cascone was born in Cleveland, Ohio, is the father of two and currently divides his time between Ohio and Michigan.

Bridget was born and raised in Southeast Michigan. She is the mother to a rambunctious boy and an avid fan of The Office.

CPSIA information can be obtained
at www.ICGtesting.com
Printed in the USA
FSHW020735150619
59067FS